Champlain and the Silent One

Kate Messner

North Country Books • Utica, New York

Champlain and the Silent One

Copyright © 2008
by Kate Messner

ISBN-10 1-59531-050-9
ISBN-13 978-1-59531-050-7

Cover Painting by Gail Smith Schirmer
Illustrations by Martha Gulley
Design by Zach Steffen & Rob Igoe, Jr.

Library of Congress Cataloging-In-Publication Data

Messner, Kate.
  Champlain and the Silent One / by Kate Messner ; [illustrations by Martha Gulley].
    p. cm.
  Summary: In the winter of 1609, with his people starving, the Innu Indian called
Silent One must overcome his reluctance to speak and trust Samuel de Champlain
and his Frenchmen in order to save his brother and regain his own spirit.
  ISBN-13: 978-1-59531-050-7 (alk. paper)
  ISBN-10: 1-59531-050-9
  [1. Montaignais Indians--Fiction. 2. Indians of North America--Québec
(Province)--Fiction. 3. Champlain, Samuel de, 1567-1635--Fiction. 4. Selective
mutism--Fiction. 5. Canada--History--To 1763 (New France)--Fiction.] I.
Gulley, Martha, ill. II. Title.
  PZ7.M5615Ch 2008
  [Fic]--dc22

                              2008029271

North Country Books, Inc.
220 Lafayette Street
Utica, New York 13502
www.northcountrybooks.com

Acknowledgments

Writing historical fiction is a journey in itself—one best undertaken with much support. I am thankful for the work of the Lake Champlain Maritime Museum, particularly Sarah Lyman, whose Champlain Quadricentennial education program will help bring this era to life for so many young people. The good people with the Clinton-Essex-Franklin Library System patiently handled my unending requests for interlibrary loans, and Social Studies teacher extraordinaire Mal Cutaiar offered his expertise on Samuel de Champlain and the world of New France. I am grateful for—and in awe of—the writing and scholarship of Joseph Bruchac, who helped review this manuscript for historical and cultural accuracy. These experts helped immensely; any errors or misrepresentations that remain despite their vigilance are my own responsibility.

I'd also like to thank Julie Berry, Judith Mammay, Candice Hayden, Gail Lenhard, Stephanie Gorin, and Marjorie Light; my writer friends who met this manuscript

Acknowledgments

at various points along its voyage, made it stronger, and helped it on its way.

Illustrator Martha Gulley breathed life into this story with her incredible sketches, and my mother, artist Gail Smith Schirmer, worked tirelessly to make sure the Silent One in the cover painting captures the spirit of the story. My father, Tom Schirmer, read early drafts, emailed me many versions of the cover, and made dinner while Mom painted. Many thanks, as well, to Zach Steffen, Rob Igoe, Jr. and everyone at North Country Books, for bringing this story into the world.

Finally, thanks to my family, Tom, Jake, and Ella—for reading drafts, sharing research trips, exploring, believing, and laughing. You make my journey wonderful.

Chapter 1

On the 5th of February, it snowed violently, and the wind was high for two days. On the 20th, some Indians appeared on the other side of the river, calling to us to go to their assistance, which was beyond our power, on account of the large amount of ice drifting in the river.

–Voyages of Samuel de Champlain

"*Ishkutshuan*—" My brother, Brave One, grabs a pine sapling and pulls himself to stand, though his knees buckle. He stares into the river.

"*Ishkutshuan*—" It is our word for a place in the current where the ice does not form. Brave One points to the one spot where the water flows freely. Nearly the entire river has turned to stone this winter.

He looks across the water. "*Mitshim*—"

Food.

He can barely raise his arm, but he points to the wooden buildings where the one called Champlain takes shelter for the winter.

Our people came to this place to hunt. We thought animals would be plentiful. We journeyed many days from our village by the north river. We watched in the season of falling leaves, as Champlain and his men packed their dwellings with seeds, beans, and barrels that they brought in their giant canoes from beyond the horizon. They call this place Quebec and give their buildings the name Habitation.

Inside those buildings, there is food.

"*Mitshim*—" Brave One drops his arm to his side but still stares across the raging river.

He is right.

It is our only chance.

The older men know. Those who are strong enough pull themselves up to lean on frozen trees along the shore. Others crawl toward their canoes on hands and feet, like the raccoon. Some drag themselves over the frozen ground on their bellies, like the snake.

I can still stand. Just barely, if a tree is kind enough to hold me up. I have seen twelve winters, and winters are always hard. But I have never gone this long without food. Hunger gnaws at my belly like a wolf, but there is nothing to eat.

Nothing.

My uncle, Singing Bear, was one of our strongest hunters. Without him, we have barely made it through the cold season.

The dried eel has been gone since the moon was new. We can no longer find the beaver. The water is too high. We have eaten our dogs and cut pieces from the furs that keep us warm. We chew them and force down bits of animal skins.

Anything to give us a bit of strength.

But our strength is waning like the moon. The oldest and the youngest have already gone to sleep and will not wake.

Those who remain have come to the river, though it is impossible to cross. The current is swift and tosses huge blocks of ice like children playing ball.

"*Ishkutshuan.*" Brave One points to the spot in the river where the fierce wind has cleared an opening, where the water flows free of ice all the way to the other side. On the opposite shore, four of Champlain's men stand watching us.

We call to them, but they shake their heads. They will not come.

The river is too treacherous.

They know.

I know.

I do not speak. I let the older men push me ahead. My mother, Crying Wren, staggers forward. My baby sister, Quiet Rain, rides in a cradleboard on my mother's back. We load the canoes. Soon we will launch, and the ice will come back to crush us.

I know.

I know because I see things. I always have.

When I was younger, the elders named me *Uhumish*, Little Owl, for I had visions. Sometimes, I would see in dreams when our enemies the Iroquois were to raid our village. I would warn our chiefs.

They know that dreams are true.

They listened.

They gathered our warriors so we were prepared, so we were watching when our enemies came. With waiting arrows and spears, we sent them fleeing, back to their river to the south. Back to the lake between the mountains.

The last time they came, two winters ago, they captured Singing Bear. They took him when they left, and my mother cried for her brother for five nights. My uncle was a brave, big man who raised me. My father died on a hunting trip before I was born, so I never knew him to miss him.

Singing Bear, I miss.

I told them the raid was coming.

I had seen it in my dream.

I told Singing Bear I had seen him carried off in the mouth of a giant wolverine, its pointed teeth sinking into his sides. I told him I had seen his burial hut, lonely in the woods.

But he shook his head.

"I must go, but I will return." He smiled down at me. "Promise to look after your mother and sister while I am gone."

"And Brave One, too," I promised, even though he is two winters older than me.

"Brave One, too. Sometimes, he has too much courage, so perhaps he will need the most looking after of all." Singing Bear laughed and squeezed my shoulder.

I promised.

And he went.

He did not return.

I still see things. I still dream. But no longer do I speak.

Chapter 1

To my people now, I am not *Uhumish*—but Silent One. I have swallowed this name deep into my belly and own it. Silence has become a part of who I am.

And so I stumble with the others from tree to tree, toward the canoes. The women climb in first, and the men push off into the frothing waves.

The wind stings my eyes like a swarm of hornets, and tears freeze on my cheeks. A rough hand pushes me forward. I stumble into the last canoe as my brother steps in and pushes us off from shore. The ice of the shallows cracks and crunches under our weight. Finally, we slide into open water behind the other canoes.

I cannot feel the paddle in my hands, but I pull it through the water, wrestling against the current. The small crowd of Frenchmen on the other side has grown. They have called their friends to come and watch the river swallow us up.

In the front of our canoe, my brother shouts something, but his words fly off into the snow before they reach my ears. The wind grows stronger. It changes direction, and the waves on the river clash and swirl.

We are halfway across, halfway to the Frenchmen and their shelters and their bread, when the ice closes in on us. Nothing has melted for three moons. The winter has been so fierce, so long. The ice chunks that move toward our boats are not like the ones we gather from the banks in springtime and carry back to our village. They are too large to imagine carrying—heavier than a full-grown moose. Some are longer than three of our huts put together. And they are closing in.

I paddle harder, but my body is tired and angry with me. I can no longer see the far shore. Black and purple spots crowd my vision the way the ice chunks close in on us.

Our five canoes crowd together in the narrow strip of open water. Children cry on their mothers' backs. Women scream over the howling wind. I look for my mother and sister but cannot find them. Great chunks of ice nudge our canoes, clunking against them and moving away, taunting us the way a dog plays with a captured rabbit.

I push as hard as I can with my paddle, willing our canoe to move forward more quickly, to cut through the ice between us and the shore. A great gust of wind launches us forward. For a moment, I think it will take us where we need to go, but the same gust heaves a giant mass of ice and slams it into us.

The jolt throws me from our canoe just before it is crushed to pieces. I land hard on a giant ice slab and slam my head on its cold blackness.

My head throbs. I close my eyes. I feel the waves toss the ice raft under my back. Frozen snow stings my face. The women cry, and I do not know if they are in the water or with me on the ice. It makes no difference. One more gust, and the wind will fling us off into the frigid waters to be crushed by the ice closing in.

I see it happening behind my closed eyes.

But when I open them, it happens a different way.

Another gust of wind blasts down from the clouds. A giant slab of ice, the size of a small village, barrels toward us. I clench my jaw and brace for the blow, the

7

impact that will send us sliding into the river.

The ice slams into us, but instead, it lifts us up, up, up—and throws our ice raft onto shore. For a moment, I expect the river to reach up with icy hands and claim us again, drag us back into its churning water. I watch with wary eyes, but the ice does not return.

A baby whimpers, and I dare to hope. I push myself up and turn. My mother clings to my sister.

I take a deep breath and let it out.

We slither off our ice raft, exhausted. The Frenchmen stare.

I look up into their pale eyes.

I look over at their dwellings and know what waits inside.

Mitshim.

They have food.

We are saved.

For now.

Chapter 2

As they were making their cabin, they discovered a piece of carrion, which I had thrown out nearly two months before to attract the foxes, of which we caught black and red ones, like those in France, but with heavier fur. This carrion consisted of a sow and a dog, which had sustained all the rigors of the weather, hot and cold. When the weather was mild, it stank so badly that one could not go near it.

—Voyages of Samuel de Champlain

Brave One plunges forward. He slips on the ice and flails his arms to regain his balance. His legs barely support his body, what little there is to support. The Frenchmen stare, and when I look around at my people, I understand why. We are little more than skeletons, clamoring at their doors for food.

They provide.

Champlain barks orders to his men. Though some of them are ill, they jump to follow his commands. I do not understand what he says. The interpreter, the boy called Etienne, is not to be found. But Champlain's words are words to save us. His men bring bread and beans from the storehouse, and we eat.

My fist is full of beans, and I stuff them into my mouth, trying not to let even one drop to the ground. They are not cooked, but it does not matter. It has been so long. We devour the food in minutes, and our chief motions to the Frenchmen to bring more. They look at Champlain, who shakes his head, and look back at us. Their eyes dart from one gaunt face to another.

One of Champlain's men stumbles as he heads back to his wooden shelter. He vomits, and blood stains the snow. Our chief calls again for more bread, more beans, and motions to the storehouse, the largest building in their small village. They shake their heads, and though my stomach cries it is not yet full, I understand.

This winter has been long. The man who stumbled off to the village is sick, and there must be others. They, too, are running out of food.

My brother's friend Steps Too Soon calls to us, and we follow. He has found the carcasses of a dog and a pig, thawing in the snow. My belly churns and pleads for food, but this meat is not good. It will make me spill my stomach onto the snow like the Frenchman.

I shake my head, but Steps Too Soon calls us forward with the loud voice of a crow. Many follow him. Hunger pains must cloud their judgment, for this boy is not a leader. He is one with a reputation for actions without thought.

Steps Too Soon received his name three winters ago when he ventured onto the beaver pond before it was fully frozen. Singing Bear found him, barely alive, in waist deep water, nearly frozen into the ice himself. He steps before he thinks. Onto the ice. Into plants that make a rash. Into trouble.

But "Come!" he calls. And today, they follow.

I stay back and watch them dig with greasy fingers and rip chunks from the body of the dog. Someone has started a fire. They thaw the flesh of the pig and devour it, half cooked.

One of Champlain's men rushes to the fire. He shouts at us and shakes his head, but we do not understand his language. His words sound like they are stuck in his teeth. Finally, Etienne, the boy who knows our language, rushes out from among the buildings.

"The meat is no good. It will make you sick," he says, and I am sure he is right. The stench from the rotten flesh burns my eyes and grows stronger as the meat thaws over our fire.

Steps Too Soon grunts at him and tears off another piece of flesh to fill his mouth. He does not understand. I step forward and raise my hand for him to stop. I point to the smoking meat. I rub my stomach to make a motion for sickness. Steps Too Soon snorts, and bits of meat fly from his lips. He shoves me back, and I stumble into Etienne.

I step back and raise my hands. There is nothing I can do.

"It is carrion—rotten meat they use as bait for the fox. They put it out two months ago. It is no good!" Etienne coughs. He is not hungry enough to understand how something that stinks so much could be a meal. He looks at me. Again, I raise my hand to the fire. I cannot stop them.

I watch the women reaching into the flames, grabbing shreds of meat for the children on their backs.

"They will be sick. It will make them weaker," Etienne says again, but he steps back, coughing, from the stench of the feast. His words have risen off into the sky like smoke. My people will eat until only bones remain.

"Aaooo!" A whoop goes up from the woods nearby, and our men leave the fire to rush over. Another young man has found the carcass of a dog, high in an oak. Two crows pick at it with sharp black beaks.

Steps Too Soon wraps his legs around the trunk of the tree and begins to climb, but it is not long before he slips back down to the snow. Too weak. Others try, but their bodies refuse to climb.

Finally, Steps Too Soon staggers off and returns with one of the Frenchmen's axes. He hands it to another man, who has strength left to use it. With feeble arms, he swings the ax. Again. And again. And again. Finally, the tree falls with a "*Whoosh...Thump*" into the snow, and the men and women swarm to the top where the dog is lashed to a branch, probably left by the French as bait like the other dog and the pig. The men whoop and chant and carry it back to the fire.

"Eat!" Brave One holds a chunk of flesh under my nose, but I turn away. I will not be sick this night. I will be needed. I will need to be strong to heal the others. Because that is what I do.

It was this gift of wisdom I received from Singing Bear before the Iroquois took him away. The gift of my healing.

Singing Bear stood before the fire the night of the feast two winters ago, when we gave thanks that illness had been driven from our village.

"Tonight," he called out over the fire, "we recognize my nephew, our little owl, as he grows into a man. We recognize his gift to our people." The drum beats and chanting grew louder with agreement as my uncle spoke.

"For though he is still young, he has shown respect for the plants of the forest, the plants that heal us, and they reveal themselves to him. He has sung the medicine chants with me, and we have driven out the spirits that spent this long winter in our village. Our *Uhumish* will be a Medicine Man. The spirits speak to him. I will be gone to the spirit world one day, but before I go, I will show him my ways so that you may come to him when you are in need of help."

He said he would teach me.

And he started. But he could not finish before he went to the spirit world.

Still, I go to his burial hut, and I ask for help.

When Singing Bear was brought home to our village, the men and boys dug a pit for his body. The women gathered his things—the kettles he had traded with the French, his furs, his axe, his bow and arrow, and arranged them in the pit. They wrapped Singing Bear in his best fur robe. Brave One and I laid his body in the pit and covered it with earth and furs. The men of our village dragged many large pieces of wood on top.

We cut saplings and built a hut over it. We covered it with shingles but left small windows.

And there it was. The burial hut in the forest. The image from my dream.

I stared in silence.

"*Uhumish*." My brother laid a hand on my arm, but I pulled away from him. "Let us leave him food and tobacco now, so that he will make the journey to the spirit land."

I pulled from my pouch the dried eel and venison, the tobacco leaves, and I pushed them through a window. But I would not speak until my brother left.

"Uncle," I whispered into the birch bark that covered the hut, "you taught me the plants of the forest, the ways to heal our people when they are sick or hurt. You taught me to speak of my dreams that the people might learn. Why did you not listen?"

I leaned against the hut to feel the smooth, cool bark. A knot in the wood scratched my cheek so it bled.

"What good are dreams, then, if the people do not listen? I spoke of my dream, and still you are gone."

I waited for an answer.

I waited until the sun returned to the sky the next day.

The wind blew through the trees. Though I listened for new messages, all I heard was the memory of Singing Bear's last words.

Promise to look after your mother and sister while I am gone.

And Brave One, too.

I had promised.

I returned to the village, silent, my own spirit broken, and I did not speak. That was two winters ago.

I have grown so tall now the name Little Owl would no longer suit me, even if I'd kept it. But when I returned from my uncle's burial hut, with my throat too full of tears to speak, my people began to call me by a new name.

I am Silent One.

I speak out loud only to my uncle, only at his burial hut. At first, I believed he would hear me, believed he would help me and teach me. I believed he would still speak, still lead us.

But as I see what is happening to our people, it is hard to believe in anything.

My brother tears the last of the dried skin from the dog, licks the stinking grease from his fingers, and leans back to close his eyes.

For now, all is well. The fire crackles, and he is fed.

But his stomach will wake him soon.

And the dog in the oak will have his revenge.

Chapter 3

The scurvy began very late; namely, in February, and continued until the middle of April. Eighteen were attacked, and ten died; five others dying of the dysentery.
—Voyages of Samuel de Champlain

The sun has turned the sky pink and red, and still I hear them retching and moaning in the huts we built last night. Champlain gave us bark to cover the huts, and so we slept for a few hours, smoky and warm inside, before the illness began.

Brave One is the sickest, perhaps because he had the most to eat. All night, I have sat by the fire and brewed the hot bark drink to calm their stomachs, but I am worried that some of them were already too weak. I fear their bodies cannot withstand this storm.

The Frenchmen are sick as well, and their leaders come to me for healing plants. I am sitting by the bench where Brave One sleeps, shaking with fever, when the boy translator Etienne sweeps aside the skin that covers the door and enters my hut.

"They say you are a healer," he says, out of breath. "Can you give us something for our fellows? A dozen of them are down now, and it seems another falls sick each morning. They can barely move. They vomit blood, and they grow weaker by the day."

I know this illness. It sometimes comes to our village in the season of snow, when we have been inside for two or three moons, eating only the eel and beaver we've dried for the winter. There is a tree, the red cedar, whose needles make a hot brew to drive away the spirits that cause this illness. I have seen it near the Frenchmen's settlement.

"Will you come with me to the Habitation?" The boy Etienne gestures toward the door of my hut. Brave One's body convulses under my hand, and I pull the furs up over his shoulders to warm him.

I look up at Etienne, but I do not answer. He knows by now not to expect it. I search his light eyes to try and find my way.

Should I follow him?

Should I go to the Frenchmen's Habitation?

We have all heard stories of our people being kidnapped by the French in earlier times. I look at the boy Etienne, wrapped in his skins, shivering still from the wind that howls outside. He is beginning to look like one of us.

I nod at him, and pulling another beaver skin up over my brother's heaving chest, I go.

When we enter through the gate in the palisade and step into the first building, I am shocked to see so many Frenchmen are down. They moan in their beds, sweating and shivering in the draft that comes through the cracks in the wood. Five of them huddle in one room, and they look like they will leave for the spirit world before the sun sinks below the hills.

I am always amazed that such a weak-looking people came here. The French are not strong, like us. Some of them have folds of flesh and marks on their faces from disease. The first time we saw them with their leader Champlain, Brave One and I laughed at how ugly they were. We picked plants and put them at our chins so we would look like them, with hair on our faces like animals. I am more accustomed to the Frenchmen now, having seen them about in this season of ice, but I still stare at their eyes, blue and green, and wonder how they could be real.

A man coughs in the bed nearest me, and blood dribbles from between his lips.

"He loses his teeth." Etienne pulls the man's jaws apart like you would handle a dog. His gums are swollen and bleeding, and there are black spaces where three of his teeth have fallen out. His gray eyes stare at me, and I turn away. It is not my job to heal the Frenchmen.

I am about to tell this to the boy Etienne, when I hear the voice of Singing Bear.

"The healing plants know when your heart is true," he told me one day as we gathered roots deep in the woods. "A healer does not turn away when there is pain."

I turn back to the man in the bed, and his dog eyes turn up to the ceiling. He mutters words I do not understand.

"He is praying to our God," Etienne says. "He prays

for an end to his pain. Can you help?"

I can. And my heart says I must.

I look up at Etienne and nod. I will return.

I leave the Habitation for the edge of the forest, where I saw the cedars with the healing needles. They show themselves to me as soon as I step into the woods, and I know Singing Bear is with me as I gather the lowest branches. I leave some tobacco leaves at the base of the largest tree in the clearing, to give thanks for the healing leaves and to show respect so that the plants will continue to offer themselves to us when we need help.

When I arrive back at the Habitation, a tall Frenchman towers over Etienne. A scar stretches from his top lip to his nose, and he squints at the needles in my hands.

"What is that? What are you giving him?"

I hold the needles out so he can see, but he is not satisfied.

"What plant is that? Will it harm him? How do we know you're not trying to poison us?"

I ignore him and reach for the copper kettle next to the fire. It is already filled with water from the melted snow. I add the needles and hang it over the flames. Soon, the aroma of the needles steeping fills the cabin with a pungent steam. Just breathing it quiets the men in their beds.

Etienne has stepped back to give me space, but the other man stares at me the way a fox stares at another fox that has strayed too close to its den.

"What did you put in the kettle?" He rises to come

toward me and reaches for the kettle, but a deep, barking voice stops him. Their leader, Champlain, steps in, slams the door closed behind him and stomps his snowy boots on the planks. I cannot understand his words, but they must be powerful. They quiet the man immediately, and he skulks out of the building.

Champlain looks at me and steps up to the fire. He lifts the lid from the kettle and breathes in the steam. He looks to the men in their beds, then turns to Etienne and speaks before leaving the cabin. The door slams shut behind him. Etienne turns to face me.

"He told me to thank you. He asks that you please do what you can for our men who suffer and promises that we will repay your kindness when you must next fight the Iroquois. We are your friends."

Friends. I stir the kettle over the fire and consider his words.

One of the Frenchmen calls for the drink, but it is not ready. Giving it to him now would be a mistake. He would be sick.

I leave it on the fire and settle back with Etienne, who sits quietly for a while and then puts a hand on my shoulder.

"You shall see, Silent One, we are powerful friends to have. Your enemies have never seen our great guns. They will be frightened. 'Montagnais friends have strong magic,' they will say. We are your good friends indeed."

The brew is just about done. He motions toward the kettle and hands me cups to fill.

I hold a steaming cup to the lips of the man in the

first bed and lift his head so he can drink. I do not speak, but I look at Etienne, who is helping the man in the next bed. They fed us when we crossed the frozen waters, and now, they offer to help us fight our enemy when the ice leaves the river.

Friends. I believe Etienne tells the truth about what his leader said.

We shall be friends.

Do I trust his words?

They feel warm but weak, like a broth that has not steeped long enough over the flames.

A fit of coughing in the next bed sends a blood-tinged spray across the cabin, and I shudder.

Will we be friends?

The snow and wind rage outside. We will all have to survive until the snow melts to find out.

Chapter 4

On the 8th of April, the snow had all melted; and yet the air was still very cold until May, when the trees began to leaf out.

—Voyages of Samuel de Champlain

Brother Sun greets us this morning. Our long winter ended with the new moon, but still, I am surprised to see his face. There were so many nights when my hunger woke me, so many days when I stumbled in weakness. I was not sure I would see the snow melt.

But this morning, the sun warms the soil. The shad run in the river again. We pull in great nets of them to dry and smoke. The women gather wood for the fire. The children run and kick the deerskin ball in the clearings.

And here I am.

Here we are, those of us who remain. Myself. Brave One. Our mother, Crying Wren, her new husband, Wise Elk, and remarkably, our baby sister, Quiet Rain.

Steps Too Soon survived his night of illness from the bad meat. Others did not. Red Bird and Quiet Deer were too weak to endure such sickness.

Only the strongest are left.

The Frenchmen, too, have lost many. Twenty-eight stayed to pass the winter here. Eight remain. The boy Etienne is among them. He approaches our cabin in the morning sun.

"Good day," he says, and I raise my hand to greet him. He is thinner than he was before the long winter, yet his spirit seems stronger. "Champlain sends for you this morning."

I turn and look behind me next to the hut. To whom does he speak? When I turn back, he laughs. "You, Silent One. He wishes for you to accompany us on a journey to Tadoussac, near your village, to meet with Pont Gravé."

I turn to go into my hut, but Etienne reaches for my elbow and pulls me back. "Please," he says. I stare into his eyes.

I look for lies, but I see none, and so I listen.

"Champlain will keep his promise to you. He wishes you to understand he is a friend. We know the Iroquois have been your fierce enemies for many years. We know you must seek revenge for their raid on your village—the raid that took away your uncle. We are interested in seeing this Iroquois land to the south. We will go with you to fight them. We will help. Our trip north is to make arrangements, and we wish for you to come, along with Brave One, and Steps Too Soon, and your war captain, Wise Elk."

Brave One and Steps Too Soon approach us, carrying lines thick with beaver pelts. Their clubs are covered with blood and fur. They have been hunting for many days, though we do not need meat. There is no hunger in our midst, now that the fish run in the rivers again.

In Brave One's eyes, though, I see a new kind of hunger—a craving for the goods that the French bring, for their metal axe blades and copper kettles in which one can heat water right over a fire. He hunts with a new thirst, seeks more and more furs to trade. He and the others raid whole beaver lodges, the way we raid an enemy village.

The beaver is not our enemy, though. He is our brother who gives himself up for us so we may live on his meat. Killing more than we need does not please the Creator. I tell Brave One this with my eyes so he can see my disapproval. But I am the younger brother. He turns away and spreads his furs on the ground to show Etienne.

Steps Too Soon does not turn away. He circles in on me like a prowling coyote.

"We missed you on our hunt, Silent One." He tears one of the beaver pelts from the line and tosses it to me. A bloody tail slaps against my thigh when I catch it.

"Oh, but you do not seem pleased that we have hunted so well." Steps Too Soon draws his mouth into a frown to mock me. I drop the fur and turn to go.

"Wait!" Steps Too Soon moves in front of me, and his wide shoulders block my way. I stare into his chest. He squints down at me and his words are whispered arrows.

"You think you are above this? With your visions and wise ideas? You are a fool. A silent fool! Leave Brave One to be a man with the rest of us while you hide in your hut and talk with your spirits." He snatches the fur from the ground and walks off.

"They are good furs, yes?" Brave One spreads out his last beaver pelt for Etienne and pulls a dried shad from his pouch. He takes a bite and speaks as he chews the tough fish. "What news do you bring from the Habitation?" Brave One is fascinated with the French and their ways. He spends hours watching them split wood and grind corn, scurrying like ants amid the buildings of the Habitation.

Etienne tells him about Champlain's journey, tells him we are called to accompany him. Brave One looks at the pile of furs at his feet, and I can read his thoughts. Kettles. Beads. Spears. An opportunity to trade.

"Tell Champlain we will go. We will be ready to leave in the morning," Brave One says and runs off.

"Excellent!" Etienne calls after him. "I shall tell Champlain immediately." He is ten paces away from my hut before I realize that it is done.

I will be accompanying the French on their river journey to arrange for the war party.

I will be one of them. So many times, I heard the stories of Singing Bear when he returned from a war party. Now, I will have stories of my own. If I return.

I hear Brave One and the others shouting hunting cries in the distance. They are after more furs for the voyage we will soon take.

I wonder many things. If the voyage will be difficult. If this is the right path for me to take. I wonder what

Singing Bear would say if he were here.

He is not. And my path is set.

In a flurry of hunting chants and a swinging of stone hatchets, my decision has been made for me.

Chapter 5

Immediately upon my arrival, Pont Gravé and I had a
conference in regard to some explorations which I was
to make in the interior, where the savages had promised
to guide us.

—Voyages of Samuel de Champlain

The Frenchmen pay him respect and call him Pont
Gravé. He is the leader of their settlement on the
Saguenay River.

We call him Stinking Dog. He is like an old dog, fat
from overeating and sleeping too much and clouded
always in a terrible stench because he passes wind all
day long.

He is louder than the men at Quebec and laughs a
deep, rumbling laugh that shakes the flesh of his belly.
He talks as much as he laughs.

Through his many words, translated by Etienne for
our chief, we hear the beginning of a story, the beginning of a promise kept. We share the Frenchmen's food,
and our war captain agrees to their plan.

We will lead Champlain and his men on an explo-
ration of the interior. We will show them where the

rivers run deep enough for their boats, and where they run so rough and fast through the rocks they would smash them into twigs. We will show them where to cross through the woods to avoid the falls, where to make camp, and where to find food. We will lead them to the country of the Iroquois, our enemy. And then, we will attack.

The Frenchmen will be powerful allies. They have not only swords and arrows, but also guns—great, noisy sticks that belch smoke and fire and can kill a man from far away. Champlain carries one such weapon, almost as tall as he is, which he calls an arquebus. It makes a great booming sound like the closest thunder, yet one cannot see the metal that flies from it until it hits its mark.

The great fire stick is powerful.

The Frenchmen promise it will destroy our Iroquois enemies.

The Frenchmen make many promises.

When we return to the settlement at Quebec, there is much excitement as we tell the news. The Frenchmen share their promises and their food, and our people take their hands in friendship.

Our warriors ready themselves for the journey up the river. They load birch canoes with dried fish and venison and ground corn that we traded with the French. We will mix it with water to make porridge when the hunting is not good.

When it is time for us to launch, Champlain takes his

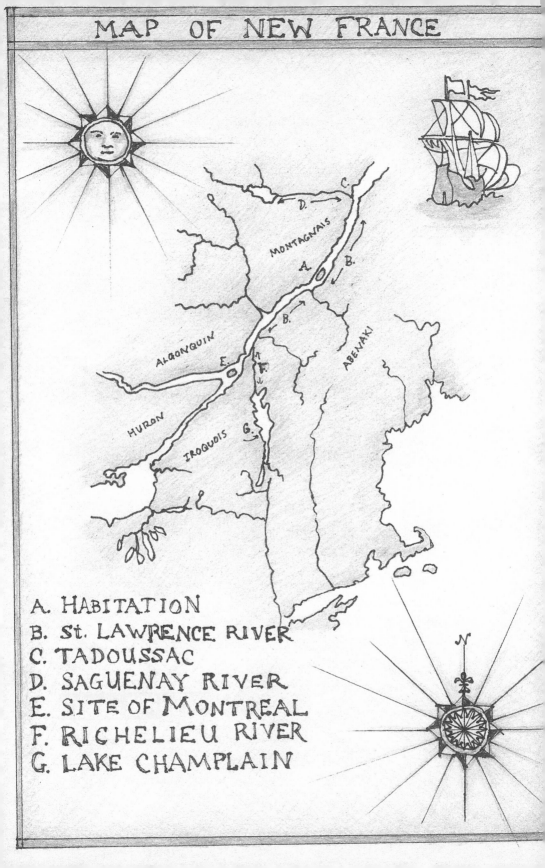

MAP OF NEW FRANCE

A. HABITATION
B. St. LAWRENCE RIVER
C. TADOUSSAC
D. SAGUENAY RIVER
E. SITE OF MONTREAL
F. RICHELIEU RIVER
G. LAKE CHAMPLAIN

men in the shallop. It is larger than our canoes, with two sails.

Our canoes are covered in the bark of the birch tree. Ribs of white cedar make them light but strong. I have heard there are rapids between here and the country of the Iroquois. If there are, we will have to leave our canoes and carry them on our shoulders through the woods. Champlain's boat is too large to carry on his shoulders. When I imagine him trying, I laugh, too. He will have to leave his boat and travel with us. Perhaps this is what our leaders want.

It is time to push the canoes off the bank. Though there are few of us, we are strong. Etienne says Champlain is expecting more help—our allies the Algonquin and the Huron, who hate the Iroquois as much as we do. They, too, have fought over hunting territory. They, too, have lost fathers and uncles to Iroquois arrows and spears.

But no one hates the Iroquois like Brave One. Since he and I pushed off in our canoe with Steps Too Soon, he has talked of battle. Instead of paddling, he sharpens his arrows and his spear.

"Can you taste their blood yet, Brave One?" Steps Too Soon has a wild look in his eyes, as if he is the one who sees visions. Brave One looks out over the water and nods.

Steps Too Soon keeps paddling but looks back at my brother to feed his anger again.

"They killed your uncle," he whispers over the waves.

"We will show no mercy, as they showed no mercy

to Singing Bear," Brave One promises. He drops his arrowhead into the bottom of the canoe and begins to paddle again.

My eyes sting with tears, but I do not speak.

We both miss Singing Bear.

I miss him with no words at all.

Brave One misses him with too many words, words that burn too hot, too fast.

"I will bring back their scalps to the burial lodge as an offering, and Singing Bear will be pleased."

Will he? I wonder. Singing Bear went with the warriors to fight, because that is what our men do. We have battled the Iroquois over hunting territory as long as I have been alive, perhaps as long as the earth has been alive. It is what we do. But I never heard Singing Bear wish for killing.

What would he say to Brave One now? He would tell him to go, no doubt. To be brave and strong. To protect his people.

But would he want revenge? I never heard him speak of revenge. Instead, when we walked through the forest to find the healing plants, he spoke of looking forward.

"Look, my nephew," he said to me once as we gathered the roots of the blue cohosh. It was just before my mother gave birth. The powder of the root would help her have the child without pain. "When you gather the roots from the forest floor, you must always leave some to grow. Never pull them all."

I looked at him but did not speak. I knew he had more to say.

"You must not think only of what happens today or tomorrow," he went on, "but of what will be here for your children, and the children of your children, and their children, as well."

I have heard these ideas many times, but it is the voice of Singing Bear on that day in the woods that I remember.

Another voice—louder—shatters my memory.

"I cannot wait to bring an Iroquois scalp back to our village." Brave One keeps paddling with the rest of us, but his heart is already in battle.

"They deserve no less," Steps Too Soon says, splashing the water with his paddle. "No less than what Singing Bear endured."

The fish I ate at sunrise rises in my throat and burns my mouth, as I imagine Singing Bear's scalp paraded into an Iroquois village.

But revenge, to me, also has a bitter taste.

"Fool! Speed up!" A sharp voice bursts from one of the canoes ahead of us. The young man we call Voice of a Crow yells at his companion, Touches the Sky, a tall, lanky boy paddling slowly in the back of the canoe. Touches the Sky keeps his pace but flicks Voice of a Crow with a splash of water.

Voice of a Crow raises his paddle and cuffs Touches the Sky on the side of the head. Touches the Sky lunges forward, and the canoe tips. Both young men plunge into the river. It takes them a long time to get back in their canoe, moving forward.

Chapter 6

The country becomes more and more beautiful. There are hills along the river in part, and in part it is a level country, with but few rocks. The river itself is dangerous in many places, in consequence of its banks and rocks; and it is not safe sailing without keeping the lead in hand. The river is very abundant in many kinds of fish, not only such as we have here, but others which we have not.

–Voyages of Samuel de Champlain

Despite some setbacks, we have made good progress, and food is plentiful. My stomach has not forgotten our long winter, and it is thankful.

The Frenchmen collect roots and berries in the woods. They do not mind doing the jobs of women. They even gather firewood when they are at their settlement.

The river has narrowed somewhat. It is not too deep here, so Brave One and I build a dam to catch fish. We make a line of stones across the current with stakes sticking up from the bottom of the river. Among the stakes, we weave branches to form a net to trap the fish. There are no people who live on these banks, so the fish are plentiful, and it is not long before we have some trapped. Brave One jabs his spear into the water to pull them out while I scoop up more with a net.

When we return to our camp, the others have made a fire and built a stand for smoking the fish. We smoke tobacco and breathe in the good smells of night.

Champlain joins our group and says something I cannot understand to our war captain, who grunts and turns away. Champlain looks for the boy who interprets and speaks quietly to him.

"He wonders why you must fight the Iroquois," Etienne says. He dips his bowl into the venison pot and begins to eat. "He says he will help you, as he promised. He will keep his word. But he wonders if you have tried to make peace."

Our warriors grumble. I do not need to move closer to know what they say.

Ridiculous.

The Iroquois have been our enemy since the beginning of the earth. How can there be peace?

Etienne does not need to understand our language to know his idea has not won the hearts of our leaders. "I understand." He reaches for more venison. "But Champlain says it would be better for you if you would make peace. It is better to settle things with words instead of having revenge."

At this, I cannot help but laugh, and I am not alone.

"The great French chief does not act the way he speaks," says Brave One, and he is right. Champlain's mouth says that revenge is not good, but his actions have spoken otherwise.

According to one of Etienne's tales around the cook fire, not long after Champlain arrived and built the Habitation, a plot was discovered. A locksmith named Jean DuVal had spread lies about Champlain and enticed four other men to join him in overthrowing the leader of the French settlement. They would wait to find Champlain unarmed and strangle him, DuVal planned, or they would raise an alarm at night and shoot Champlain when he came out. DuVal promised riches to those who helped him. He would get rid of Champlain and turn the settlement over to enemy fur traders.

One of Champlain's men, a pilot, told him what was happening. When he found out about the plot, Champlain demanded the names of those involved.

The French leader is a wise man, a crafty one. He sent the pilot with wine for the men involved in the plot, invited them to a party in the woods. When they were weakened from the drink, he seized them and threw them in prison.

Champlain executed the leader of the conspiracy by hanging, impaled his head upon a pole and displayed it in the most prominent spot in the fort.

This, from the man who says it is better to settle things with words.

Our war captains frown their disapproval. They cannot abide a man who is not honest, a man whose actions do not match his words.

Champlain comes again to speak with Etienne, and the boy nods as his leader walks briskly toward the boats.

"He says he understands. He will offer help as he said he would. He says he is a man of his word."

Wise Elk says nothing, but takes a fish over to the boats and hands it to Champlain, who takes it and nods.

A gift has been given and accepted, an understanding forged.

The next morning we set off as the sun rises red over the mountains. It has been hot. The air is thick and wet, and insects come in swarms to pick at our flesh. I smear my skin with bear grease to keep them from biting.

The smallest flies, tiny black spots with wings, are the worst. They ravage us, and we bleed from their wicked bites. How strange that one so small can inflict so much damage. The tiny flies are strong warriors indeed.

We shall have to be like the flies when we encounter our enemies. So few Frenchmen are left from the winter, and so few of us have come on this journey. What if the Iroquois village is large? What if they have many warriors?

I look at our line of canoes. It does not stretch very far.

Our paddles pull us around a bend in the river, and suddenly our numbers have grown.

Camped near an island the French call St. Eloi are swarms of Ochateguins and Algonquins—our friends in battle against the Iroquois. Champlain does not know this yet. He reaches for his arquebus, but our war captains call out, and Etienne tells Champlain he will not need his weapon.

"Do they have a chief?" Champlain asks, lowering

the gun back down into the belly of his shallop. "Take me to their chief."

"Paddle this way." Etienne motions me toward the shallop, and he and Champlain climb into our canoe. It sits low in the water with the added weight, but the river is slow here, so we are still safe. "Take us to shore, to see their leaders."

We pull the canoe on shore, and I turn back to look at the others, waiting out on the river, watching to see what happens.

Champlain turns to the men who are beginning to step out of their cabins. "Your chief?" he asks them. He shows his sword, lifts his own helmet, a sign of his distinction. Then he points to them again. "Your chief?"

A boy about my age steps forward.

"Yroquet…Ochasteguin," he says, reaching for Champlain's hand to lead him. The Frenchman's white flesh glows pale against the warm brown of the boy's fingers.

The boy leads Champlain to a hut, just like ours, and pulls back the skin covering the door. Inside are not one but two chiefs. They welcome us to their cabin.

With Etienne's help, Champlain tells them of our voyage so far, of our plans to meet the Iroquois and do battle. I am not sure how much of the story was understood, but the chiefs look pleased by the time Champlain lifts the deerskin again to leave.

Later, more Algonquins come to the shallop, bringing furs. Champlain gives them copper pots and glass beads. They smile and laugh and take their goods back to their huts, looking at their reflections in the shiny copper.

The next morning, the two chiefs call for Champlain. They wish to speak with him again, but when he comes, they are quiet for a time. They smoke tobacco and whisper chants. Finally, in loud voices that can be heard by all on shore and on the river, they speak.

"Almost ten moons ago, the son of Yroquet visited this man at his dwelling, and he gave a good reception to our people." They look at Champlain, who is looking at Etienne to translate, but the chiefs speak too quickly. "He told us then that he and the other Frenchman on the river to the north would fight with us against our enemies. This man is true to his words. He is here now to help us, just as he said he would come." They turn to the other men of their tribes on shore. "And so we call for you to join us, all, to make an alliance with this Samuel de Champlain and his men."

There is a thundering whoop, and the men rush forward. Champlain still does not know what was said. His eyes widen with fear, but he shows courage and stands still. Finally, Etienne finishes speaking in his ear and he nods.

"There is one thing more," Etienne adds. The chief Yroquet is still talking and pointing back down the river. "They wish to go back to Quebec first."

"Back to Quebec?!" Champlain puffs up like a bear one comes upon in the woods. "Why ever would we go back when we have come this far up the river already? We'll not go back to Quebec! They'll join us from this point on. They cannot—"

The chiefs step in closer. Their eyes narrow. Though they do not understand Champlain's words, it is clear they understand his disrespect. Others begin to circle around as well, their faces darkening.

"They cannot—" Champlain stops again and looks at the shifting figures around him. He looks down the river, then back at Etienne. "Why do they wish to return to Quebec?"

"They wish to see your settlement there, and also—"

"A grand tour? For God's sake, they—" The chiefs step closer, their eyes searching Champlain's face. His eyes meet theirs, and his shoulders drop.

"Go on," he says to Etienne.

"They wish to see what our houses look like, and they wish to see how our weapons work. They say it is right that you do this."

Yroquet takes a step back and speaks a few more words to Etienne in a quieter voice.

"And there must be a feast. Then, he says, after three days, we will all come back to show you the country here and fight."

"Very well." Champlain steps briskly back to the canoe at the water's edge. We scramble to climb in, and he follows. His boot lands so hard in the boat I think he might punch a hole through the bottom, but when he pushes us off, the canoe does not take on water.

"We shall depart in the morning."

Our paddles cut through the water and churn it into pink waves as the sun sets over the forest.

Chapter 7

The next day, we set out all together for our settle-
ment, where they enjoyed themselves some five or six
days, which were spent in dances and festivities, on
account of their eagerness for us to engage in the war.
　　　　　　　　–Voyages of Samuel de Champlain

We pull the canoes onto shore by the Habitation, and
the other Frenchmen come out to greet us. They talk all
at once, like ducks and geese, until finally Champlain
holds up a hand to silence them. He speaks. I turn to
Etienne, but he shakes his head. He has been told not to
interpret, that Champlain speaks only to his own men
now. I offer him a piece of smoked venison from my
pouch. Etienne is skinny as a stray dog and always hungry.
He laughs and accepts my bribe.

"Very well," he says, chewing the salty meat. He
lowers his voice and gazes at Champlain, holding court.
"Champlain tells them that the savages wish to see how
civilized men live. He says they are here to see the settlement and to see that they are friends. To that end,
Champlain says his men should trade with the savages
fairly and provide them with many colored beads and

copper kettles."

I watch as Champlain lifts a string of beads into the air, laughing.

"But no guns."

I am not surprised. Champlain and the others carry the fire sticks they call muskets and arquebuses close to their chests and sleep with them at night. They are very precious to the Frenchmen and contain strong magic. I do not wish to fight. But if I must, I am glad this magic will be fighting with us instead of against us.

There is a great roar of laughter from the Frenchmen.

"He tells his men to enjoy the dancing and feasting, as it may go on for some days," Etienne says. "He says the savages promised to depart in three days' time but are famous liars and so it may be winter before the voyage continues."

The Frenchmen disperse in their cloud of rowdy laughter. They scurry like insects gathering bread and meat and barrels of rum to bring to the fire. I wonder how they can say one thing in front of us and something so different when they do not intend for us to hear their words.

I step through green leaves onto the quiet moss of the forest floor. I kneel by a fallen tree to look closely at white mushrooms that grow from its rotting trunk. Some are good to eat, but others will make a man's head swirl in sickness.

These are no good. So I move on. Some things look fine but are poison inside. It is good not to make decisions too quickly.

When the feast begins, the deep smell of roasting venison fills the air and almost lifts me from my feet. We are not hungry like we were in the time of snow and ice, but we have traveled long days, and our bodies need nourishment. The meat simmers and spits over the open fire. Fat crackles with sparks above the flames.

My mother brings another kettle full of water to set over the fire. My sister toddles along at her feet. Her chubby fingers hold the handle of the kettle, too.

My mother will make a stew of forest plants and turkey the hunters shot when the sun was high in the sky. They brought the birds back in both hands, laughing about the stupid turkeys that do not fly away when one bird is hit by an arrow but sit waiting for their own turn.

My mother pries my sister's fingers from the kettle, hangs it up, and raps the shiny copper with her knuckles. "It is good to cook this way." She nods toward the Frenchmen across from her on the other side of the flames.

She is still amazed at this copper pot that can sit directly in the flames. It is so much faster than heating water in our pots of clay. We could not put them on the fire or they would shatter. Instead, we would heat rocks in the fire and then drop them, steaming and hissing, into the water in the pot until it was warm enough to cook. The meat was never cooked all the way, not like it is with the copper.

"I am thankful to our neighbors for the kettles," my mother says.

"Be thankful to the beaver," Etienne laughs, as he

and Brave One arrive, their faces glowing red and orange in the flickering flames.

"*Missi picoutan amiscou*," Brave One says, and they laugh. The other young Frenchman with Etienne does not understand.

"It is their little joke about how productive the beaver is, when they trade their furs with us," Etienne explains. "*Missi picoutan amiscou*. The beaver makes kettles, hatchets, swords, knives, bread…"

It is true. The furs that are so plentiful here are like gold to these men from across the waters. At first, I did not understand how it could be so, why they would trade us so much for such common furs.

"They are valuable in France, across the sea," Etienne explained to me when he visited our lodge one day. "There, we have hunted the beaver until there are no more to be found. The men of Paris still clamor for beaver hats." He ran his hand over a fur spread across my mat. "Your furs here are better than those to the south. They are fine, and they bring a good price back in Paris."

I still do not fully understand. I am not sure any of us understand. Yet we have come to need the Frenchmen's copper kettles. My mother adds roots to the stew, and I inhale the sweet steam.

"My stomach is ready, even if the stew is not," Brave One says, reaching past me to dip into the kettle.

But Steps Too Soon rushes in, almost knocking it off the spit. I have to grab Brave One by the shoulder to keep him from toppling over into the hot coals.

"Look!" Steps Too Soon holds out a wooden bowl and then dips his finger in. When he pulls it out, the tip is stained a deep crimson. "I have brought war paints."

He dips all of his fingers from one hand into the bowl where he has crushed roots and berries. When he draws out his hand, his fingertips are red. He smears them across Brave One's cheek and leaves angry red streaks behind each finger.

Brave One's eyes seem to come alive as the paint smears his cheeks. He takes the bowl from Steps Too Soon and holds it out to me.

"For Singing Bear," he says, and so I reach into the wooden bowl.

The warm, sticky paste sends prickles through my fingertips. I helped Singing Bear paint his face on the night before he went off on the raid. I still see him in my mind's eye; the red slashes stained his face like blood.

I wipe my hand on the grass and step back from the fire. The wind shifts, and smoke burns my eyes to make tears.

I miss him.

I wonder what he would say if he were here tonight. Here to smell the good smells of tobacco and roasting meat. Here to consider the Frenchmen's plans to explore down the lake until we find our enemy. Here to listen to the pounding drums that beat with our hearts in excitement and in fear.

Mother stirs the pot. My sister finds a stick and beats on the kettle like a drum. Brave One, Steps Too Soon, and Etienne tear hunks of meat from the deer, belching and laughing. I rip off a small piece of meat and take a pinch of tobacco leaves.

They will not notice I am gone.

On quiet feet, I walk away from the fire, then break into a run as I approach the edge of the village and Singing Bear's burial hut. It is dark, but my moccasins know the way. They have traveled this path many times.

"Uncle," I whisper and step quietly up to the hole in the shingles. The breeze blows, and the leaves whisper back to me.

He is here. He listens.

I pull the meat and tobacco from my pouch and poke it through the opening in the shingles, an offering to show respect, to show Singing Bear that he is not forgotten at our feast tonight.

"Uncle," I whisper again, and I stop. It has been so long since I last spoke to my uncle, so long since I last spoke at all, perhaps my voice has left me. Or perhaps I do not know where to begin. How do I explain that I am lost among my own people? I wonder if Singing Bear sees my brother, the hold that Steps Too Soon has on his spirit, his fast friendship with the French boy Etienne. How he changes.

"Brave One has not forgotten you either," I whisper into the shingles. "But he remembers you now with anger, with a heart for revenge. I do not have that heart of courage. When I think of fighting the Iroquois, my stomach threatens to leave my body, and my heart beats in my throat. I am afraid," I admit.

"Whooo!" An owl calls from a pine bough high

overhead. His yellow eyes reflect the fire at the center of the village. Drums and voices rise on the night wind and find me, even here.

"The Frenchmen say they wish to help us fight our enemies. The men who took you from us," I whisper. "Should I go?"

I wait for an answer.

But the owl is silent. The leaves do not speak.

Finally, soft footsteps shush through the pine needles.

"Silent One, you must return to the feast." My mother walks up to the burial hut and runs her slender hand over the bark shingles.

I look at her but do not come.

"Singing Bear's spirit will be with you when you dance."

Quiet Rain stirs in her cradleboard on my mother's back. She reaches up for a pinecone on a low branch.

"Come," my mother says. "Your brother waits for you."

I follow her through the trees. I look back and listen for words from the clearing. But my answer is not there.

It lies ahead of me.

With a mother who steps on quiet feet. A sister clutching a pinecone in her hand. A brother who prepares for war.

And a promise to protect them while Singing Bear is gone.

Chapter 8

*...their chiefs said...that as a token of firm friendship
and joy, I should have muskets and arquebuses fired,
at which they would be greatly pleased. This I did,
when they uttered great cries of astonishment, espe-
cially those who had never heard nor seen the like.*

–Voyages of Samuel de Champlain

Sharp cracks like thunder echo through the trees
before us as we walk back to the fire. My baby sister
whimpers.

"Shush, little one," my mother says, reaching back
over her head. "Shush..."

Wise Elk appears among the trees and takes my
mother's arm to lead her back to the fire. My sister
reaches out to pull his hair, and he laughs. He is a good
father to her, has been a good husband to my mother
these past two winters. And he would like to care about
me, I know. But when he looks into my eyes, he sees
the shadows of the fathers I have lost. First my own
father. Then Singing Bear. And for now, there is no
opening for light.

There is another boom from the clearing, followed

by great whooping cries of approval. As we step back into the center of the village, smoke pours not only from the cook fire, but also from the muskets in the hands of four Frenchmen. The Algonquins who met us on the river to the south stand with their mouths open as if they are drinking in the gray clouds of smoke. Their eyes are wide open and they motion for more.

"Now…" Champlain steps forward lugging a gun larger than all the rest, nearly as tall as the Frenchman himself. "You shall see why we will be victorious over your enemy."

He pours black powder from a horn into the pan of the great gun, hoists it up, and puts his finger on the small piece of metal in the middle of the gun. With the smallest motion of the finger, a thunderous boom echoes off the cliff. It vibrates in my chest like a thousand beating drums.

The Algonquins have never seen the Frenchmen's guns before. Some stare. Others jostle about, poking one another with fingers and elbows. They let out whoops and cries.

A feeling of power has settled on our people with the smoke from the Frenchmen's guns and the weight of their promises. They say their great guns can kill three men with one shot. They say we will soon destroy our enemies. They say we will soon taste victory.

Soon.

But for tonight, there is bear meat and venison, eel, fish, and beaver. There are roasted roots, and tender green shoots that taste like morning dew.

And for tonight, there is dancing.

The drums have grown louder since the final blast of the arquebus. They carry us through the night on sure, steady footsteps. The firelight dances, orange and gold, on the cliffs, as if it, too, hears the music of our feast. The voices of my people are one, chanting with the drumbeat. Their song carries off over the trees, over the moon, and into the darkness.

My feet want to join the dance. My mother's gentle push on my shoulder moves me forward into the circle, and I begin to move. I hop twice on each foot, keeping time with the drums, keeping time with the heartbeat of our village.

Some move in small circles, small steps in time with the drums. Others twirl and whirl like the flames. But all in the same time. Together. We are one.

Brave One twirls twice into the center of the circle, his big feet pounding the earth. He has grown. Our warriors look at him and speak softly to one another. He will fight well. He will not turn away from danger. They know.

So do I.

My brother will fight bravely. And I made a promise. I cannot let him stand alone.

As my feet pound the earth, I hear in their beat the voice of Singing Bear. I know what is to be when the dancing is done. When the feasting is through, the drums fall silent, and the fire fades to embers, we will go to war. Brave One will paint his face as a warrior and sing chants with the others. They will gather war

clubs and spears, bows and arrows. They will launch their canoes.

And I will be with them.

This dance tonight is not so different from my dreams. I dance the dance of a warrior, and my heart beats a wild mix of excitement and terror. I know what the raids are like. I know what I am about to face. I see my future in the smoke rising from the fire. Like my dreams, this vision is as clear as the midday sun.

Like my dreams, it will come, whether I speak of it or not.

Chapter 9

On the 28th of the month, we equipped some barques for assisting these savages. Pont Gravé embarked on one and I on the other, when we all set out together. The first of July we arrived at St. Croix, distant fifteen leagues from Quebec where Pont Gravé and I concluded that, for certain reasons, I should go with the savages, and he to our settlement and to Tadoussac. This resolution being taken, I embarked in my shallop all that was necessary, together with Des Marais and nine men.

—Voyages of Samuel de Champlain

I am not the only one who is silent today. Perhaps it is our weariness from the days of feasting. Perhaps it is the thoughtfulness that comes before a raid, as a quiet sky precedes a storm. Perhaps it is the thought of more burial huts to build, more brothers to visit in quiet places in the woods, when we return. Our paddles slice through the waters with quiet gurgles and drips, but our voices are silent.

We are a larger group now, two or three hundred, plus the Frenchmen. The one from the north, who the

French call Pont Gravé and we call Stinking Dog, the one we visited with Champlain, has joined us.

For three days, we have paddled from the sun's first light to the end of day. At night, we stop to make camp, and our hunters go into the woods along the water to find food. Even our cook fires have been quieter since the feast, as we wait for what comes.

Tonight, small circles of men chatter around the fire. Etienne rips a piece of meat from a rabbit roasting over the flames and lowers himself onto the soft grass next to me.

"Well, my friend, we are about to be a smaller war party." He bites into the meat, and grease drips down his chin. He does not have hair on his face like the others yet, but there are a few short stubs on his chin that glimmer with shiny beads of fat in the firelight.

I poke a stick into the fire. The orange coals spark when I turn them over.

"Tomorrow, Pont Gravé and many of the others will depart in the barques." Etienne points to the small ships that have sailed alongside our canoes. "Champlain will keep fewer than a dozen of us."

I leave my stick in the fire and look at Etienne with a question in my eyes.

"Don't worry, I will stay, my friend." Etienne pushes himself onto his feet but pauses. He squats, staring into the flames.

"I am more one of you, I think, than one of them," he whispers, then rises to walk back toward the little knot of Frenchmen who whisper and laugh raucously at even turns.

His comment makes me laugh when I look at the pale skin of his hands and the beginnings of a beard on his chin. But Etienne wishes he were a part of our world, rather than theirs. He has more of our spirit than Champlain's. He is different from the others. Sometimes, when the fire was dying out back at our village and my people would go to their huts for the night, I would watch him. He would watch the fire until its last embers faded, watch our backs until the last one disappeared under the deerskin that covers the door.

It was not his world, he knew. But I could see, even then, that he wished it were so.

I fall asleep with the fire warming my face. When I wake the sun burns red through my eyelids.

As I rise, the Frenchmen make final preparations for Stinking Dog's return to his settlement. Most of his men will go with him. But Etienne, as he promised, is among those who will stay.

When we climb into the canoes this morning, Champlain and his men pile into just one boat—a shallop much smaller than the barques that will travel back to the north. I am called upon to help move their supplies on board. I try to keep my distance from the Frenchmen. They smell horribly, as they rarely bathe. My mother is always amazed they can make such beautiful things—the shiny copper kettles, the shimmering glass beads—and yet be so stupid and dirty.

As I put down a barrel on the deck, one of the

Chapter 9

Frenchmen sneezes. He pulls a fine linen cloth from his pocket, empties his nose into it, and stuffs the filthy rag back into his pants. It makes my stomach churn. I am happy to finish loading and step back into my canoe with Brave One and Etienne, who paddles with us.

We are about to push off when Steps Too Soon takes an awkward step into our canoe and almost tips it over.

"You would not leave me behind, would you, brothers?" Somehow, he smiles warmly at Brave One and Etienne while glaring at me, like a two-headed monster from one of the stories our elders tell in the dark.

We push off again, lower in the water with Steps Too Soon's long body folded into the canoe between Brave One and Etienne. With four of us paddling, though, we soon glide through the ruffling waves.

Today, there is a different feeling in the cool air. A sense of moving forward. When I peer over the side of our canoe, the faces that reflect back at me are more confident and sure. Etienne is the first to give voice to what I sense.

"We are drawing nearer. The fighting will be good. We will show your enemies how powerful we are together."

He is confident Champlain will lead us to a quick victory.

But when I try to hold my chin high like the others, it feels forced. My stomach is tight, and not from hunger. From fear. A voice in the wind tells me this raid will not be as simple as the Frenchmen think. Nothing is.

The Frenchmen believe in their great guns like we

believe in our gods. But these guns are difficult to fire. A single arrow from Brave One's bow might go straighter and farther. And I wonder if Champlain truly understands the fierce nature of the Iroquois.

Etienne frowns at me. I wear no masks, so he can tell I have doubts.

"You do not know Champlain as I do," he says, pulling his paddle from the water and resting it against the side of the canoe. "He understands matters of war. He fought in the Royal Army in France, an army larger than your greatest villages here. He has come here to the New World many times and visited the place we call the West Indies with his uncle."

"I have heard talk about this place," Brave One says, still paddling. He pokes Etienne with his paddle, and Etienne dips his own back into the water. Reach, pull, lift. Reach, pull, lift. The easy rhythm of our strokes calms me. I watch trees slip past on the banks. Nut trees and birches that will give way to elms as we move south. And I wonder about the trees that Champlain must have seen on his other journeys, south of here.

"It is an amazing and beautiful place, with clear blue waters and islands thick with plants of every kind." Etienne tips his head into the sun and breathes in. "Always warm. Not like our wretched winters in this place.

"Champlain loved it, but he hated the way the Spanish treated the savages there, taking them as their slaves and kidnapping them." He looks at me. "That is why he wishes to be a friend to you."

I look over my shoulder. On the deck of his shallop,

Champlain shouts orders to his men, strutting about like a bird showing its plumage. He clearly believes himself to be above the rest of the Frenchmen, the way he sticks out his chest in his fancy clothing and tips his head in his feathered hat.

I do not understand this idea that one man could be above another. We are all made of the same clay. Brave One once told Etienne the same thing.

"But you have your chiefs," Etienne said to him. "And they are set apart by their belongings. They wear shining copper ornaments in their hair and on their wrists. They are above the rest of the men. It is the same."

But it is not. The trinkets worn by our leaders are not signs of superiority, but of strength. They show these men can provide for their people. That is their highest hope.

Champlain tips his hat back from his eyes and looks at our canoes. He says something to one of his men, adjusts a sail, and nods. We are moving forward more quickly, swept along on wind and words and promises.

I do not know—I cannot see—how this raid will end. But I can feel that it is coming soon.

Chapter 10

Thence we continued our course to the entrance of Lake St. Peter, where the country is exceedingly pleas-ant and level...We passed a large number of islands... Fish are here more abundant than we had seen. From these islands, we went to the mouth of the River of the Iroquois, where we stayed two days, refreshing our-selves with good venison, birds, and fish, which the savages gave us. Here there sprang up among them some difference of opinion on the subject of war, so that a portion only determined to go with me, while the others returned to their country with their wives and the merchandise which they had obtained by barter.

–Voyages of Samuel de Champlain

No one dreams.

Not even me.

It is not a good sign.

Before a raid, as we approach the enemy, we wait for a dream. One of our medicine men, a seer, will dream that the enemy is at hand, and we will prepare for bat-tle. Most often, I am the one who sees it first. But we have reached the River of the Iroquois, and they should be within a few days paddle from us. I have had no dream.

Each morning when we wake, the other men search my face with their eyes. They find nothing. I have had no vision, and I worry that my gift of seeing is gone. Has it followed my voice off into the clouds?

Our warriors grow impatient.

Some, like Steps Too Soon, dream of tasting our enemy's blood. Some, like Brave One, dream of revenge and will never turn back. But these are not the dreams for which we wait.

Some of the Algonquins who joined us for the trip back to Quebec for the feast suggest it is not the time to make a raid.

We build our shelters on the shore, build a wall around them on three sides, and spend two nights in this place. The forest is full of plants with tender leaves and filling roots. The skies are filled with waterfowl, and the waters swim with fish of every kind.

We eat well.

We sleep well.

But we do not dream.

On the third morning, I wake to voices louder than the usual mutterings of dawn. I step out to see canoes pushing off. Half of our warriors, perhaps more, are leaving. The pink morning light reflects on the river, rippling into purple and gold as their paddles push them away from us. Away from the raid on our enemy.

"Cowards!" Steps Too Soon scoffs and spits into the shallow water at the river's edge. "They came only to trade their furs for the Frenchmen's copper and glass.

They are not true people of the dawn." He claps his hand on Brave One's shoulder and pulls him in. "It is up to us now, Brother." Brave One had been watching the canoes with a look on his face that I could not understand. But as Steps Too Soon pulls him closer, it disappears. Confidence returns to his eyes, and he turns away from the canoes. They slip away in a river of shimmering light.

My soul paddles off into the sun with them. I wish I could go. What good am I here? A warrior with no stomach for battle and no voice to hold it off. A seer who has no visions.

But then Brave One steps up beside me. His shoulder brushes mine, and Singing Bear's voice returns to me.

Brave One, too.

Sometimes, he has too much courage, so perhaps he will need the most looking after of all.

I remember why I must stay.

Chapter 11

No Christians had been in this place before us; and we had considerable difficulty in ascending the river with our oars. As soon as we had reached the fall, Des Marais, La Routte, and I, with five men, went on shore to see whether we could pass this place; but we went some league and a half without seeing any prospect of being able to do so, finding only water running with great swiftness, and in all directions many stones, very dangerous, and with but little water about them.

—Voyages of Samuel de Champlain

Sixty of us remain, and we paddle on.

We have reached a place where the water flows quick and shallow. It bubbles over sharp rocks and spills over falls. I have not seen this part of the river before, though I know places like it. We pull our light canoes onto the bank for the night. Tomorrow, we will lift our boats from the river and carry them on our shoulders through the woods until we find quieter waters again.

Though the canoes are all on shore, Champlain has not joined us. He stands at the bow of his shallop and frowns into the churning white water. His boat is clumsy and heavy. It will not fit on his shoulders. He knows this and motions to his men. They disembark and set off into the woods.

I pull flint from my deerskin pouch and strike it to make a spark. Brave One and Steps Too Soon bring dry grass and coax the fire to join us.

"I hope we meet our enemies soon," Brave One says, arranging the smallest twigs into a pyre over the smoking grass.

Steps Too Soon blows on the pile, trying to fan it into flames, but only scatters the dry grass into a smoky mess.

"It cannot happen soon enough for me." Steps Too Soon scoops the hot grass back into a pile. He burns himself on an ember, whips his hand away, and sends the twigs flying. "We must take scalps in trade for Singing Bear's." He brushes the grass and twigs together again.

Brave One nods. "It is time."

He strikes the flint to cast another spark onto the grass.

A breeze brushes through, and the flames fan up in a sudden whoosh. We feed the fire with thicker branches until it is large enough for smoking.

Etienne brings a fish he speared from the waters with the help of some others who made a dam to trap them. Etienne has learned our ways as quickly as he has learned our language. Perhaps it is because he has fewer winters, and the language of the Frenchmen is not stuck so deep in his throat.

"Where have Champlain and the other men gone?"

Brave One asks, setting up the sticks so they will support the fish. Its scales sparkle in the firelight like colorful glass beads in the sun. Soon the fat begins to drip, crackling and hissing into the fire below. The smell of roasting fish fills me with hunger.

Etienne does not speak at first but holds out his cup. Brave One shares with him the thick porridge we made by mixing water into the ground corn. He dips his spoon into the paste and fills his mouth.

"They search for a new route through the woods." Specks of porridge fly from between his lips, but he continues. "The shallop cannot travel these waters. You must have known that." He swallows.

Brave One smiles. There is corn meal stuck in his teeth.

Etienne turns the fish and looks to the river, where the shallop is coming ashore alongside our sleek canoes. With its clunky wooden sides and tilted mast, it sticks out like a moose among a herd of deer.

"They've returned," Etienne says. "I will be back shortly." With quick steps, he goes to meet the men as they gather back at their boat. He stands frowning as Champlain speaks, then nods his head and points to the part of the river where the water runs fastest. He moves his head from side to side, and Champlain's eyes narrow, but Etienne speaks again. This time, he points the other way, back toward Quebec. Champlain's eyes follow Etienne's pointing arm, and finally, Champlain nods and steps back onto his boat. He is talking quietly with one of his men when Etienne returns for his fish.

"What was the talk?" Brave One asks, tearing a

chunk of white flesh for Etienne. He knows food will buy information.

"They're going back," he says simply.

"No!" Brave One's eyes pool with angry tears. "They cannot go back! We are so close. I know it! Any night now, one of us will have the dream."

"They will not all go." Etienne bites into the fish. "Owwf!" He pants like a dog, hanging his burned tongue out into the cooling night air. Brave One laughs.

Etienne blows on the fish, a cool wind from between his tight lips, and takes another bite. "Champlain will keep his word to you. But he is not pleased. You told him the rivers would be no problem and his shallop could travel the whole distance. This is not possible."

"We told him nothing." Brave One offers no more fish, but stares at Etienne with a challenge in his eyes. It is true. Our people never promised Champlain his shallop would carry him all the way to the home of the Iroquois. But it is also true we did not tell him all we knew about the rapids. We did not tell him his shallop would never make it the full distance.

"Regardless," Etienne says, "he cannot continue with the shallop. The others will take it back to Quebec, and we will continue in your canoes."

"Who?" Brave one narrows his eyes.

"Champlain and some of his men."

"How many?"

"Two."

Brave One's eyes burn with anger, and I understand why.

This is the tremendous aid in battle promised by the Frenchmen? Two men and their leader against numbers of Iroquois we cannot know? Etienne does not notice Brave One's anger, or he chooses to ignore it.

"Champlain will stay with his guns, and that is all that we will need against the savages," he says, reaching for more fish. Brave One does not stop him. I reach for some of the soft, white flesh, too, and it flakes into my mouth. I lick fish oil from my fingers, and the sun slips behind the hills.

I hope Etienne is right and the raid will be over quickly.

But I am afraid because I have not had a vision to tell me what will come. At the same time, I am afraid of what I might see. Before the last raid, I knew what would happen.

Trying to stop it was like standing up to stop the wind.

In the morning, the men on the shallop lift anchor and start back to the north. Champlain steps with a clunk into our war captain's canoe, and his weight pushes it down in the water. Still, it floats.

Etienne climbs in with Brave One, Steps Too Soon, and me. I am glad. He will paddle and pull his weight through the waves.

Most of the supplies went back with the other Frenchmen, so we travel more quickly. When we reach the point where the waters churn too violently for us to pass, we pull our canoes up onto the bank and lift them over our heads. Others carry bows and war clubs and baskets of food and skins.

Finally, we reach a place where the river flows with a quieter spirit, and we put our canoes back in the water. Etienne and his friend Nicolas continue alongside us on land, while Champlain climbs into the canoe with Brave One, Steps Too Soon, and me.

We paddle silently for a time, the four of us. The landscape holds great beauty. It reaches into my chest and quiets my heart. Champlain gazes at the shore, then looks at me and points back to hills the color of sunset that roll in the distance.

I nod, content to slip quietly through the day, drinking in thick leaves and rocky shores. But the Frenchmen are rarely content with quiet. Champlain looks from Brave One, to Steps Too Soon, to me and speaks.

"Les arbres sont tres grands, oui?"

Brave One looks to me and I put my hands in the air. Champlain sounds like a dog barking with food in its mouth. He knows we do not understand his words, but it seems he wishes to speak anyway.

"Les arbres…" Champlain stops paddling and motions toward the island we pass, where tall pines caress the sky. Then he stretches out his hands, leaning so that he nearly tips the canoe. *"Ils sont tres grands. Non?"*

He looks at us and waits.

I look at Brave One. He looks at Steps Too Soon and raises his shoulders. They frown at Champlain, who keeps barking and pointing and stretching.

"Atemu," Brave One says, pointing at Champlain. *Dog.*

I smile. He indeed has the blue eyes and sharp

tongue of a dog. Champlain nods and points to the island of pines again, smiling. For some reason, he is pleased.

"*Oui,*" he says. "*Les arbres sont tres grands.*"

We paddle the rest of the way in silence, and when we stop to make camp, we build shelters and a palisade around our temporary village. We will rest here for a day or two. The hunters have already brought back fowl for our meal.

When we finish, Steps Too Soon runs off to find Etienne to see if there is news. Brave One and I recline by the fire as our duck cooks. I look out past the flames.

Champlain barks at his own men now. They understand him and bark back.

I sit up on my elbows and watch the water as their language slips off into the night, past my ears that hear sounds but no words I understand.

I will share meat with the Frenchmen tonight. I will sleep beside them, like brothers. And together, we will keep watch for the same enemy.

Yet I have no words to offer them. Even if I spoke, it would mean no more to them than the cawing of a crow.

We may share a journey, but we will never be of the same tribe.

Chapter 12

After they were established in their cabins, they dispatched three canoes, with nine good men, according to their custom in all their encampments, to reconnoiter for a distance of two or three leagues, to see if they can perceive anything, after which they return. They rest the entire night, depending upon the observation of these scouts, which is a very bad custom among them; for they are sometimes while sleeping surprised by their enemies, who slaughter them before they have time to get up and prepare for defence.

—Voyages of Samuel de Champlain

Brave One and Steps Too Soon head out in canoes with some other men to act as scouts. They will travel quietly up and down the river to see if there are signs of our enemy.

Etienne joins me at the fire while they are gone.

"Ah, Silent One. Shall I keep company with you while we rest?" He raises his hand in greeting as is their custom, and I offer him a piece of dried venison. That is my own ritual with Etienne. He enjoys any tradition that involves food.

Chapter 12

"Of course, you will not answer. But that is all right, my friend." Etienne tears the venison with his teeth. "I can speak words enough for us both."

I smile. Despite how he looks, his skin the color of the birch tree, his hair the color of dried grass, this boy is so much like Brave One. Full of big words that do not quite match his size. In some ways, he is beginning to feel like my brother from another land.

I speak none of this aloud, but perhaps the breeze carries my thoughts to him, for Etienne looks at me and smiles.

"I will tell you a secret, Silent One, because with you, I know it will be forever safe." He leans closer. "I have thoughts of staying here."

I look around at the riverbank, and my brow furrows. It is not a good place for a permanent settlement.

"Not here, exactly," Etienne says, "but here in this new world, with your people, when mine go back across the sea. I suspect it is a matter of time. How can we weather another winter like the last?"

Indeed. How could any of us?

"And so," he continues, "I may not go back to France with Champlain after our raid. I would like to marry a nice savage girl." He grins a wide coyote's grin. Bits of venison are stuck in his teeth. "And live as you do." His eyes take in our rounded huts, our smoldering fires, and approaching on the river, our quiet canoes.

I think of the girls from my village at home. Little Sparrow, who loves to tie shells into her long, black hair as she walks by the river with her sisters. I think of the way she would stand watching me catch fish in the days before our long winter came. The way she would smile at me from the other side of the fire. I wonder what she would think of having a pale husband with hair growing out of his face.

My chest grows tight at the thought, and I look hard at Etienne. He gnaws at the last bits of meat on the deer rib in his hands. He might stay. But he will never be one of us.

"The woods are quiet, and we are hungry," Brave One calls from his canoe. He and the others have returned from scouting.

They climb back on shore and join us with their report.

There is no sign of the enemy. It is time to rest.

"You know," Etienne speaks in his usual loud crow's voice, now that the subject has changed. "Your plan for the night is a foolish one."

"Why do you say so?" Brave One asks, though he already knows the answer. Champlain has urged us to leave some men awake through the night, standing guard against our enemy lest they sneak up like silent cats to pounce on us while we sleep.

"It would be safer to leave some men awake, to keep watch," Etienne urges.

Brave One looks at me, and makes the motion with his hand to show that Etienne does not think clearly. To stay awake all night long would hardly prepare a man for battle. That is why we send out scouts. To ensure that it is safe for our warriors to sleep.

All day long, we are at work. Every man has a job.

We are divided into three groups. The first group of men goes ahead to watch for signs of the enemy. They look not only for enemy warriors but also for any mark left in the woods—an arrow or drawing on a rock or tree—to show that our enemies or friends have passed this way. The hunters stay behind us and off to the sides, so that they might shoot animals with their swift arrows to feed us all when we stop. And the main body of the group travels in the middle, always armed with our war clubs, our bows and arrows, always alert. Always ready to fight.

No, we will leave no men awake.

Our bodies need rest for the dawn.

Chapter 13

In all their encampments, they have their Pilotois, or Ostemoy, a class of persons who play the part of soothsayers, in whom these people have faith.

—Voyages of Samuel de Champlain

Brave One waits for Etienne in the morning and walks with him as soon as he emerges from his hut.

"Has he had a dream?" Brave One asks. He believes Champlain may be the one who has a dream to tell us our enemies are near.

So far, our own medicine man Sees with Hawks— the Frenchmen call him our Pilotois—has seen no visions. He will build a new medicine hut today.

"A dream?" Etienne stretches and scratches his belly.

"Champlain. Has he had a dream of our enemy?" Brave One asks impatiently.

Etienne shakes his head. "No dream that he's told me," he says wandering over to the cook fire. "Now, me...I had a dream. A most rare vision indeed."

Brave One waits.

"I dreamed of breakfast." Etienne grins and dips his bowl into the stew pot.

I smile, but Brave One sulks away. His mind is not on food.

Later, we are called to help with the cabin for Sees with Hawks. He is the one who has visions, the old man who travels with us and tells us when we will find our enemy. He has strong medicine and will ask the spirits when we will fight.

Brave One brings an arm full of sticks and logs from the forest, and I begin to stack them, leaning them up against one another to make a point in the middle.

When we finish, Sees With Hawks walks slowly over and nods at us. We have done good work.

He covers the cabin with robes of fur and disappears inside.

Soon, almost all of our people have gathered outside the cabin to wait for answers.

The voice of Sees with Hawks mumbles in low tones inside the cabin, but we cannot hear what he says. He speaks not to us, but to the spirits. He says when he is in his cabin, a spirit appears to him in the form of a stone and tells him whether we will meet our enemies, whether we will kill many of them.

The muttering grows louder, and the cabin begins to shake. I know that Sees with Hawks lies on the ground now, that the spirits have come.

The cabin shakes more violently.

We sit watching, breathing as one, and waiting.

Champlain and Etienne step up, talking loudly. They do not notice when everyone's eyes fall on them. The older warriors glare, and Wise Elk holds up a hand. None of us would dare speak while Sees with Hawks is talking with spirits.

Champlain finally grows quiet, glances at the cabin with Sees with Hawks closed inside, and lets out a snort of laughter.

"*C'est un jeu ridicule!*" Champlain barks, gesturing toward the cabin.

Etienne shifts his weight from one foot to the other. He looks at Champlain, then at us.

"What does he say? Has he, too, had a vision?" Brave One asks.

"No." Etienne shakes his head and pauses, biting his lip. "He does not believe your medicine man, your Pilotois. He says it is a ridiculous game."

It is not a game for the sixty of us who sit and wait. The cabin shakes. And we wait. We know the outcome of the battle depends on what Sees with Hawks learns from the spirits inside his cabin.

Champlain speaks to us again, his words spilling out quick and sharp, his hand flicking toward the tent where Sees with Hawks has grown quiet.

"He says look more carefully," Etienne translates. "He says you will see your medicine man's hand on the poles, making the tent shake."

My people buzz with talk at this idea. Impossible. Some of them raise their voices. Champlain has insulted them. Brave One talks with another tall young man, nods, and rises to come to Etienne.

"You will wait with us," he says, indicating a spot

next to him in some flowers. "And you will see. He talks with our spirits, and he will tell us when we will fight."

"Well, actually, I told Monsieur Champlain that I—"

"You will stay." Brave One's eyes challenge Etienne to refuse. It is a challenge he does not accept. He sits. And he watches.

The cabin shakes some more and finally grows still.

Sees with Hawks pulls aside the fur and steps out, blinking, into the light. "The spirits tell me we shall go tomorrow," he says. The men hang on every word. "Our enemy waits for us further up the lake. We shall go. We shall fight our enemy and kill many of them. And we shall return victorious."

The men sitting murmur and nod, all except for Etienne, who stands to leave.

"Champlain is right, you realize," he says. "No one can do what your medicine man claims he can do. No one can see the future."

But he is wrong. I close my eyes. Sees with Hawks is right. I feel, more than see, our enemy waiting at a narrow part of the lake.

"And what makes you think your spirits will assist you in battle against the Iroquois?" Etienne goes on. "What makes you think the spirits will choose a side? It is a silly notion."

Is it?

I think back to the morning's first sun, when the Frenchmen were talking on their knees outside their cabins. Etienne told me they were praying to their gods.

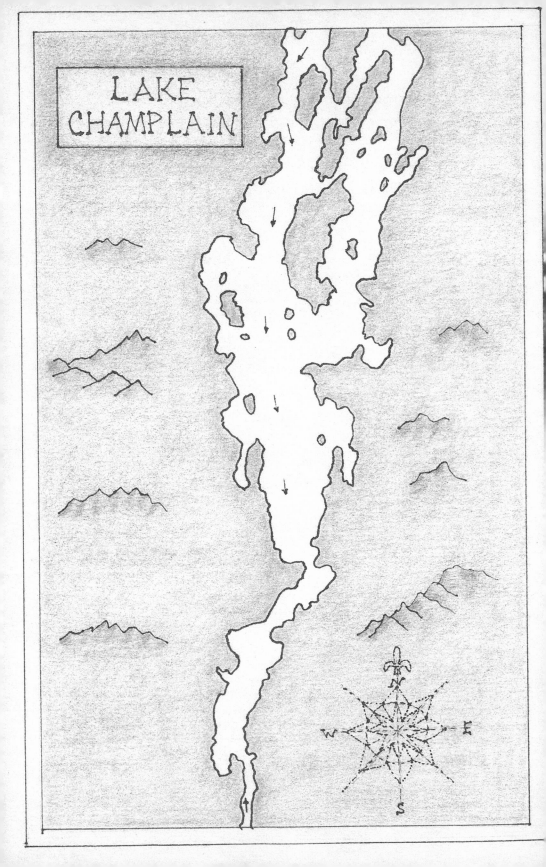

"Deliver us, Lord, from our savage enemies and keep us safe in your care. Let us be victorious and gain much land. Amen."

Chapter 14

There is also a great abundance of fish, of many varieties; among others, one called by the savages of the country Chaousarou, which varies in length, the largest being, as the people told me, eight or ten foot long. I saw some five feet long, which were as large as my thigh; the head being as big as my two fists, with a snout two feet and a half long, and a double row of very sharp and dangerous teeth. Its body is, in shape, much like that of a pike; but it is armed with scales so strong that a poniard could not pierce them. Its color is silver-gray. The extremity of its snout is like that of a swine. This fish makes war upon all others in the lakes and rivers.

—Voyages of Samuel de Champlain

We have reached the lake, and such a place I have never seen.

Our older men, our warriors, have been here before.

Singing Bear was here on two raids before his last one. He told me stories of its vastness. He told me of the mountains that rise on either side of the valley, like giants stretching into the clouds. He told me of the clear, cold waters, of the wild fowl and fish so plentiful. He told me of these dream waters.

And still, it steals my breath away as we enter the lake.

The Frenchmen are stunned by the life in this valley, and even we, who are used to the feast of animals and plants the spirits provide for us, see this place is different. The fish and fowl exist in such great numbers. Our hunters return to camp at the end of day laden with animals for our meal. There are fowl of every kind, deer, bears, and more beavers than we have seen.

The Frenchmen are most intrigued by the fish we call Chaousarou. It can grow to be longer than a man is tall and has a drawn-out snout with two rows of teeth, sharp as the point of a spear. Its body is covered in armor, like the metal plates worn by Champlain himself.

Etienne is fascinated by these fish. He keeps watch over the sides of our canoe as we paddle.

"There!" He points to one as we drift through tall grass. "It waits for a meal, I think." We stop paddling and drift at the edge of the reeds. Chaousarou lurks deep in the grass with just its snout sticking out of the water. It is perfectly still and silent.

This is the way we creep up on our enemies in a raid.

A young heron wades nearby, dipping its long beak in the weedy shallows. Chaousarou watches with eyes like the Frenchmen's beads of glass. Its knobby head looks like a tree stump sticking out of the water.

A great gull with black and white wings thinks so, too. It soars in, preparing to land on the stump, and SNAP!

Etienne startles so that our canoe nearly tips.

"Take care," Brave One says, "lest you become its next meal."

Chaousarou drags the bird, flapping and screaming, beneath the murky water. We watch until the surface is quiet once more, and we resume paddling.

Etienne keeps turning to stare at the place in the reeds. He has not known Chaousarou as long as my people have. We know the fish is a great warrior, with its quiet patience and swift attack. We know, too, of its healing power.

When one of our brothers has an injury, a sore leg or arm, we use the power of Chaousarou to heal. Three winters ago, Singing Bear taught me how to use the head of the fish. Its teeth, sharper than the sharpest stone blade, can be used to bleed a man who is hurt. When he is touched by Chaousarous's teeth and bled in the spot where he has pain, the great fish will steal away the pain.

Tonight, I dream. I dream that I am Chaousarou, waiting in the reeds. I smell the fresh grass, the cool water, the warm blood of my prey.

Two Iroquois warriors appear in the sky. They do not see me.

They fly on powerful white wings and dip low over the water.

I wait.

I am patient.

I am still.

One swoops over me to land. In a snap of my jaws

too fast for eyes to see, I devour him, but not before I, too, am pulled under the dark waters.

When I rise again, when the sun sparkles off the waves once more, the other warrior is gone.

I wait, but he does not return.

It is not over.

The creeping. The waiting. The attack.

It will never be over.

A rustle of leaves outside our cabin wakes me with a start, and I lift the deerskin to peer out into the moonlight. It is only a raccoon, searching for scraps of food left from our meal. He is nothing to fear.

Still, as I sit on the edge of my bench, my heart pounds in my chest like a trapped animal. I wished for a dream, and it came. But what a dream it was.

I saw the raid at the edge of the water. It will happen. And I will spill our enemy's blood on their land.

Color fills my eyes when I close them again—warm and dark and red.

I open my eyes and step out into the night, but the vision will not leave me. Even the moon is tinged with blood.

I look to the sky and hope for wind, a message from Singing Bear. But the air is so still it suffocates me with quiet.

I was supposed to be a healer. A visionary.

My dream says I will be a warrior.

And soon.

Chapter 15

Now, as we began to approach within two or three days'
journey of the abode of their enemies, we advanced only
at night, resting during the day. But they did not fail to
practice constantly their accustomed superstitions, in
order to ascertain what was to be the result of their under-
taking; and they often asked me if I had had a dream,
and seen their enemies, to which I replied in the negative.
Yet I did not cease to encourage them, and inspire in them
hope. When night came, we set out on the journey until
the next day, when we withdrew into the interior of the
forest, and spent the rest of the day there. About ten or
eleven o'clock, after taking a little walk about our encamp-
ment, I retired. While sleeping I dreamed that I saw our
enemies, the Iroquois, drowning in the lake near a moun-
tain, within sight. When I expressed a wish to help them,
our allies, the savages, told me we must let them all die,
and that they were of no importance. When I awoke, they
did not fail to ask me, as usual, if I had had a dream...
I told them that I had, in fact, had a dream. This, upon
being related, gave them so much confidence that they
did not doubt any longer that good was to happen to them.

–Voyages of Samuel de Champlain

We are close to the country of our enemies. We travel now only when the sun drops into the mountains.

I have told no one of my dream, but each time I wake from sleeping, Brave One asks what I have seen.

"It is near? Is it? You must give us a sign when you have had your dream." He pesters me like the flies on the riverbank and cannot be swatted away.

I try but I cannot speak. My stomach still churns and my head still swirls with my vision. He will see for himself soon enough.

The sky has turned from black to purple to pink. It is time for us to stop for the day. Time for us to slip deeper into the woods to sleep. This way, our enemy will not see us coming. This way, we will be rested when it is time to fight.

We pull the canoes into the brush and carry our baskets into the woods.

I sink down at the base of an old elm to rest, but Champlain paces here and there. Brave One, Steps Too Soon, and Etienne trip over one another at his heels.

"Monsieur Champlain," Etienne says, "do you think it will be long now?"

"Surely we are close. Ask if he has had a dream." Steps Too Soon nudges Etienne so hard he stumbles over a root and into Champlain, nearly knocking him into a patch of raspberry bushes.

Champlain turns and though I expect him to bark, he smiles and speaks to Etienne, then folds his arms and stares at them all.

"He says to tell you, my courageous friend, that he

has had no dream," Etienne says, "but he says he is sure our efforts will be successful." Etienne looks up at Champlain, who speaks quick, sharp words and gives him a rough shove. Etienne pulls Brave One and Steps Too Soon toward the patch of trees where I am resting.

"And he says to go away," he adds, as if Champlain's push hadn't made that clear.

Steps Too Soon paces among the trees as if he bounces from one to another.

"It has to be today! It has to be!" he says to the birch and the pine.

Brave One sighs and sits down with a thud on the ground next to me.

"Champlain has not had a dream." He picks at a sapling growing up from the roots of the tree. "Surely, if we were close, he would have had a dream. What if we are not to meet the Iroquois? What if this long voyage has all been for nothing?" He has shredded a leaf into pieces the size of the smallest insects, and he tosses the pieces at the elm.

"If Singing Bear were here, he would know." Brave One's dark eyes shine with tears of frustration, and I recognize the same longing I feel for our uncle. For a moment, I think of telling him about my dream, but Etienne joins us.

"Be patient, Brave One." He reaches over to pluck the other elm sapling at the base of the tree, but I grab his wrist. Our grandmother elm should not lose her children to their frustration.

"What say you, Silent One?" Etienne pulls his hand

back and looks into my eyes. "They say you have visions. They say you are the one who will dream when we are close to your enemy. Tell us. Is it so?"

I lean back into the warm rough bark of the elm tree. In my mind, I disappear. I am Chaousarou again, waiting in the cool water, amid the tall grass. I see our enemies again in the sky, and in my heart, I know they are near. They are a threat. The others need to know, too.

I brush the pine needles and bits of old leaves from the forest floor and pick up a twig to scratch lines in the dirt.

"Come!" Brave One leaps to his feet and yells through the trees. "Silent One has had a vision!" Etienne and the other men crowd me like vultures that smell death. I do not look up. I do not speak. My lines in the warm dirt speak for me.

I scratch sharp points—the pointed teeth of Chaousarou. The great fish takes shape in the shadow of the elm. Next, I draw a fallen warrior in its mouth, a warrior with the markings of our enemy.

The Frenchmen have gathered now, too, and as I scratch in the last lines, the men erupt in whoops and fast talk of battle. They leave me and run off to make plans, carried through the trees on a flood of confidence, a thirst for war.

I look down at my drawing in the dirt, exhausted. It feels like my own blood has seeped out into the earth through the drawing stick, and I can barely hold up my head.

I push myself up and wander deeper into the trees.

If I dream again today, I will dream alone.

When I wake, the pink sky has moved from the east to the west. It will soon be time to set out again. My stomach rumbles with hunger, so I walk back to where the others have gathered. There will be food.

We can no longer cook on a fire, since the smoke would show our enemies our position. But when I find the others, they are dipping into a bowl of corn meal mixed with water in a cool porridge. Brave One runs to me.

"Champlain, too, has had a dream!"

Champlain stands at the center of a circle of two dozen of our men. Etienne stands beside him, turning his head from side to side, trying to listen as many people speak at once.

Normally, our people do not do this. It is the Frenchmen who chatter all at once like shore birds. Etienne throws his hands in the air, and there is quiet. I step closer.

"Here is what you must know," Etienne translates. Champlain speaks quickly in his ear. The men lean in, almost falling over one another to listen. "He has had a dream about your enemy. In his dream, the Iroquois were drowning in a lake near a mountain." The men nod in approval and lean in to hear more.

"This mountain is within our sight," Etienne continues. The men look down the lake, where mountains tower to both the east and the west. "He says the Iroquois were drowning, and he expressed a wish to help them." Our men furrow their brows. One cries out in disbelief, but Etienne holds up his hand again until it is quiet. "But he says he did not help them because you, our allies, said they are of no importance, and we must let them all die." The men nod and look back at Etienne, who looks up at Champlain.

"*C'est tout.*" Champlain says, shrugging his shoulders.

"That is all," Etienne says, and the men start squawking again. It certainly means a quick victory, they decide. Some are concerned Champlain wanted to help our enemies, but others wave away their worries.

"Do you think it will be tonight?" Brave One says, out of breath from rushing to me. He claps a hand on my shoulder. "You will see, Silent One. We will fight like men. We will do the work that Singing Bear set out to do, and his spirit will shine down on us."

He walks off to help prepare, and only the moon shines down on me. It rose over the tallest mountain while Etienne spoke to the men.

Our warriors' voices grow louder as they load the canoes with baskets and weapons. Excitement spreads through the air like smoke from a fire.

Soon we will set off.

Soon, we will meet our enemies.

I did not need Champlain's dream to know.

Chapter 16

When it was evening, we embarked in our canoes to continue our course; and, as we advanced very quietly and without making any noise, we met on the 29th of the month the Iroquois, about ten o'clock at evening, at the extremity of a cape which extends into the lake on the western bank.

–Voyages of Samuel de Champlain

The sky has darkened to a purple gray.

We push our canoes into water smooth as polished rock. Our quiet paddles ripple the moonbeams and send noisy drips into the night air.

Even Steps Too Soon has been quiet. He stares forward into the dark.

Brave One turns back to me, and the moon shines in his worried eyes. His confidence has faded like the setting sun.

"Silent One," he whispers, watching the water drip from his paddle, "do you think we will come upon them tonight?"

I do not think. I know. His eyes plead with me to answer, and I nod.

Brave One turns to paddle again. His shoulders rise

as he takes a deep breath and sighs to the stars and the waves. He looks up at the sky. Perhaps he speaks with Singing Bear in his mind, as I speak to him at his burial place. Brave One's shoulders rise again and fall, and his paddle plunges deeper into the water alongside our canoe. He pulls with more strength, more confidence. He is ready. And so am I.

My bow rests in the bottom of the canoe against my leg. It rubs on my shin when the canoe tips in the waves, so there is a raw spot on my leg, angry and red. I do not move away. I know what is to come.

In my heart, I talk with Singing Bear and tell him why I will fight. Not for land or for revenge. I will go to stand beside Brave One. My brother will not have a burial hut in the woods so soon. We will both return home to hunt so that my mother and sister will not starve the next time the snows come.

I will keep my promise.

We paddle onward. Animal eyes glow green along the shore, as if the forest creatures know what is to come. The moon has crept higher in the sky and is almost overhead when our lead canoe stops paddling to drift on the still water.

Brave One, Etienne, and I stop paddling, too, and our canoe glides forward toward the others. When we are close enough to hear whispering, we lean toward the other boats as far as we can without tipping our own.

"They are here," whispers our war captain, Wise Elk. "See?"

He points into the line of moonlight that ripples on the water, and in the distance, I make out canoes. At least twenty.

Brave One's shoulders rise again, and I hear the whoosh of his breath leaving him. I breathe the same deep breaths of dark air, trying to take in enough courage to face this night.

"How does he know they are Iroquois?" Etienne whispers.

"The canoes," Brave One says, pointing. "The birch tree does not grow as well where the Iroquois make their villages. Their canoes are made of elm. Look how they sit lower in the water than ours."

Etienne nods. It is easy to see the difference. Our canoes are lighter and faster. I feel pride at this, but light canoes and proud hearts do not win battles. The Iroquois are fierce.

Singing Bear told stories of the Iroquois' courage in raids. Though they are our enemies, we admire their bravery and their skill.

"One day," Singing Bear told me, "it may be your time to fight, and you, too, must show courage. You must go forward when you want to turn back. You must stand by your village, by your people. The time will come when you are needed."

We drift on gentle waves and watch the elm canoes in the moonlight.

Brave One leans in to me. His heart pounds against my shoulder.

The time is here.

Chapter 17

They had come to fight.

—Voyages of Samuel de Champlain

A loud whoop erupts from the Iroquois canoes and rips the quiet air. The lake stirs. Our canoes rock and threaten to tip.

"We must prepare." Brave One nudges me. He reaches for his bow and sets an arrow into place. He lets out a shrill war cry, and his face glimmers in the light of the moon, shiny with paint and sweat. His eyes are hungry, searching the waters for Iroquois canoes that seem to have vanished. He points, and I see the canoes closer to a point of land that juts out into the dark water.

"They go ashore," Wise Elk whispers from another canoe. "Pull the canoes together."

We paddle in close to one another and tie our boats to poles to keep them from drifting off on the waves. We face them, ready to fight.

And we wait.

The Iroquois paddle closer to shore and step out onto the slippery rocks. One of their leaders, a big man wearing an eagle feather, slips and loses his balance, waving his arms like a bird flapping in the sky.

"They cannot even make it to shore without falling down!" Brave One laughs. The confidence has returned to his voice and his eyes. "Soon you will fall and not rise!" he shouts to the shore.

His taunts echo back at us.

"You shall be destroyed!"

"Your warriors are cowards!"

"Your men are afraid to fight!"

The insults fly sharp as arrows through the night. The Iroquois warriors work on shore. They draw up their canoes close to one another. Their axes thunk against trees, punctuating the jeers and shouts, as they cut wood for a barricade. The moon travels across the sky. Before it sinks into the mountains, they are protected inside their quick stockade.

Four of the Iroquois men approach us in their canoes.

We float, ready for them. We watch to see what they do.

They come close but make no move to attack.

"Do you wish to fight?" one of them asks. He reminds me of Brave One, still young, with the worried eyes of a boy but the strong voice of a man. "Will you fight us?"

My heart beats so loud in my own ears that I barely hear our response.

"We wish nothing more," Wise Elk says.

"Our chiefs will engage you, but not until it grows light." The Iroquois boy gestures to the setting moon. "It is too dark now for us to recognize each other. But when the sun rises, we shall offer battle."

"And we shall answer." Wise Elk nods, and the Iroquois men turn silently on the darkening waters, paddling back to shore to rest the night.

We rest little, for the night is anything but quiet.

The Iroquois build a great fire, for they no longer need to conceal where they are. Their drumbeats echo off the rocks, and their chants carry out to us on the lake. They dance with a kind of desperate fury, the kind of war dance I danced the night before we left to come with Champlain.

The Iroquois drumbeats take me back to the night of feasting in our village before we left on this journey. It was the last time I saw my mother, when she came to fetch me at Singing Bear's burial place in the woods, to bring me back to the feast. It was the last time I saw my sister Quiet Rain, squealing and pointing at the flames. It was the last time I spoke to Singing Bear at his burial place. The last time I spoke at all.

Hearing their chants, feeling the beat of their dance, makes me long for the fires of home. The warmth of our village huts. The faces of my mother and my sister.

"Dance well, for tonight shall be your last feast!" Brave One screams above the noise. "Cowards!" His voice cracks at the end. It is changing into the deeper song of a man but still remembers the high pitches of a boy.

The taunts volley back at us from across the waters.

"You are the cowards!"

"You should not have come! Tonight will be your last night!"

"You will run when you see our spears, our arrows!"

"We will be victorious when the sun rises!"

All night long, they dance and drum and chant. All night long, we float off shore, shouting into their circle of fire and music. All night long, our words feed their hatred, and their words feed ours.

When the sky grows light, our people's voices are scratchy and worn down.

All but mine.

But my head pounds with the noise of the darkness and dreams of what this dawn will bring.

Chapter 18

When day came, my companions and myself continued under cover, for fear that the enemy would see us. We arranged our arms in the best manner possible, being, however, separated, each in one of the canoes of the savage Montagnais. After arming ourselves with light armor, we each took an arquebuse, and went on shore.

—Voyages of Samuel de Champlain

The Iroquois have not seen Champlain.

They believe we come alone, like we usually do.

This time, we do not.

Champlain, Etienne, and Nicolas have passed the night in hiding. Even now, as we approach the Iroquois barricade, they crouch in the bottom of our canoes, clutching their great guns, waiting for the right moment to appear.

As our canoe pulls into the shallow water along the shoreline, Champlain dresses himself in armor. He looks like a turtle, tucked inside his shiny breastplate and shells.

But as he steps clanking from our canoe, he has something the turtle lacks. The arquebuse. Champlain is strong, but he can barely carry it on his own.

The Iroquois stare at this long stick as he advances. They have never before seen an arquebus. They have never heard its thunder or felt its fire.

They will today.

We follow Champlain, climbing from our canoes to take our places. Before we entered the lake, our leaders took branches and sticks from the trees of the forest and arranged them on the ground to show each man where he would be in battle.

Brave One, Steps Too Soon, and I are in the back, behind rows of more experienced warriors. I take my place beside them, remembering the sticks on the ground.

Brave One and Steps Too Soon are the maple twigs on the right. Then me. A smaller oak twig with an acorn still attached. Etienne, the birch stick, is beside me, with Champlain, a great white pine branch, and his arquebus, on his left.

We are ready.

Our enemies stream from their barricade. They, too, are ready to fight. They pour from the entrance like ants from an anthill. There are more than we thought. Two hundred, at least.

Their leaders must have arranged sticks on the ground as well, for each warrior walks slowly to a place as if it is marked, and waits. Three Iroquois war captains line up at the head of the group.

"Are those their chiefs in front?" Etienne whispers across me to Brave One.

He nods. "Not chiefs, but war captains. You can tell

them because their plumes are so much larger than the others." He points at the tall feathers at their heads. Brave One narrows his eyes. "Tell Champlain he must try to kill those three. Tell him to do all he can."

Etienne nods and whispers to Champlain, who answers him.

"He says he will do all that is in his power," Etienne tells Brave One. He turns to face the Iroquois again. They are so close, I can see their individual faces, their eyes. They are full of the same fear that squeezes my chest as I stand.

It happens before I am ready.

There is a shout. A command, but I do not hear what it is. Our warriors run forward. They advance two hundred paces or more. The Iroquois raise their bows. They pull back their arrows.

Brave One and Steps Too Soon run ahead of me, and I force my feet to follow. But the crush of warriors in front stops us.

There are war cries.

Arrows.

Screams.

But we see nothing, blocked from the battle by our elders.

"Wah-ooooo!" Steps Too Soon whoops. He surges forward but is pushed back. He throws down his bow in the dust and whirls around to Brave One.

"We come as warriors, but we do not fight!" Tears flow down his cheeks in streaks of red and brown.

"We were told to follow the older men," Brave One

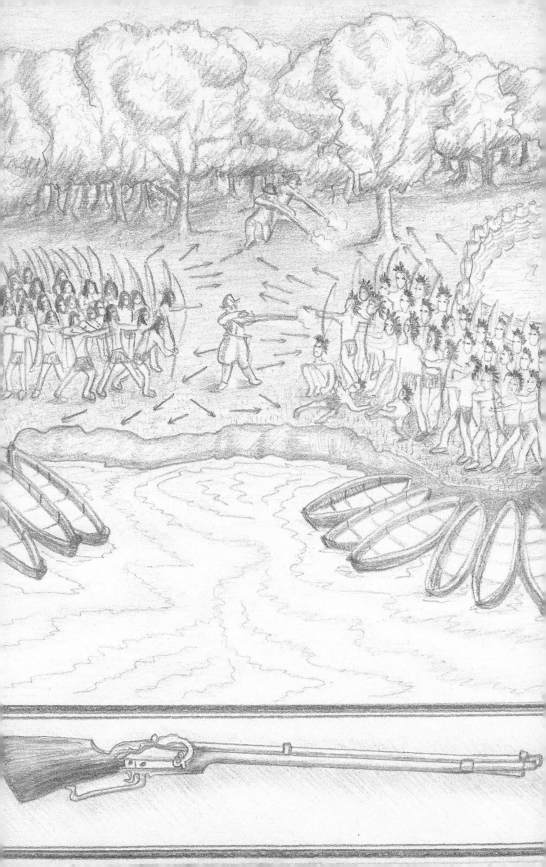

says, but he, too, strains to see the front of our lines.

"The older men do not have our fire." Steps Too Soon spits on the ground. He lunges down to pick up his bow. "They do not have our courage. Look! See how they release their arrows and sink back into the lines, cowering. This is not the way to be victorious."

He turns to my brother. His eyes are spear points. "These, Brave One, are the men who took Singing Bear from you. They deserve to die as Singing Bear died."

Another whoop goes up from the front of the line. Brave One's face flushes red under layers of sweat and dirt, war paint and tears. He takes a deep breath and plunges forward.

He shoves his way between two of our largest warriors. One loses his balance and falls over the feet of the other. Steps Too Soon trips over the fallen warrior and tumbles into the dirt.

I clutch my spear and rush forward. But I cannot get past them. When I look up, Brave One has disappeared into the crowd of bodies, swallowed up by whoops and cries of war.

Steps Too Soon rises but falls back as an Iroquois arrow flies between his shoulder and his ear. He is no longer pushing his way to the front, but seems to be sinking back.

I push past him, into the trees at the edge of the clearing where I can move forward without being seen. I duck under branches and dash between trees. I search for Brave One's short, stout figure among the men. Finally, I see him. He has plowed his way almost to the front of our lines. He stands, facing four Iroquois warriors who seem the size of pine trees—taller than our tallest men.

They stand with their bows drawn, but Brave One does not fall back. He raises his own bow. He steps forward.

"No!!" I break out of the woods after him. But a sharp hand closes on my shoulder and yanks me back. Etienne.

"Do not go," he says. "Champlain will fire now."

More of our warriors rush past. I can still make out Brave One's head at the front of our lines. Shorter than the rest of our men. Rushing forward all the same.

An arrow whistles by my ear.

I swore I would not let him go alone.

I wrench free from Etienne and leap from the woods. I fling my spear with a cry that cuts through the war noises, high and fierce. It comes from my mouth but does not sound like me.

I strain to see where my spear goes. I lose sight of it, but one of the Iroquois men facing off against Brave One falls to the ground at the right time, and I know.

I search the crowd of brown faces for Brave One, but I cannot find him.

"Fall back!" Etienne pulls me back into the trees.

A scream comes from the front of the line. Men call for Champlain.

"Come! It is time!" Their voices carry through the morning air. The warriors part and make a path to let him through.

The air, so full of whistling arrows and boastful war cries, falls heavy with quiet as Champlain steps to the front.

He faces the Iroquois leaders.

We stand behind him. And we wait.

The three Iroquois war captains stare at this pale visitor who stands in the place of our own leaders. They stare at the great gun he holds at his side. His arquebus. But they do not know its name.

One of the war captains raises his bow, but before it reaches his ear, Champlain lifts his great gun and fires into them. Two of the Iroquois leaders fall immediately. The one who had raised his bow freezes as if paralyzed by the sound and the smoke.

Or perhaps he is paralyzed by the magic.

My people have seen before how the Frenchmen fire their guns and shoot down a man without an arrow in sight. For the Iroquois, this is new. A kind of sorcery they have never seen.

The third war captain falls to the ground. A red stain spreads from the wound on his leg, and he stares. Perhaps he is looking for an arrow, a spear. Something to explain the blood and the pain. But he will find no arrow. That is the magic of the Frenchmen's guns.

Loud cries erupt behind me. Our warriors cheer Champlain. The air fills with more arrows. Soaring still on the blast of Champlain's gun, our warriors surge forward. Champlain looks down to reload.

A few of the Iroquois return our fire, but most of them stare. Their eyes dart from Champlain, to their fallen captains, to the stick that spit fire at them. It is still breathing wisps of smoke.

Another musket blast rings out from the edge of the woods, where Nicolas hides. Another Iroquois warrior falls.

It is too much for them. The noise. The wounds without arrows. The fire and the smoke.

The Iroquois turn and flee into the forest. Our men follow and give chase through the thick brush. Champlain and his men fire their muskets again and again in pursuit.

I remain back in the clearing, nearly alone.

The three Iroquois war captains have fallen in a tidy row. One of them still breathes. I snap off a twig from a willow branch at the edge of the clearing and kneel to put it in his mouth. He bites down on it and grimaces in pain, but he chews. He spills too much blood onto the ground. The wound on his leg will kill him. There is nothing I can do for him, except give him the willow to dull the pain.

I stand and look back at our canoes, waiting. I take a few steps toward them and trip over something in the taller grass. I catch myself and look down.

It is Brave One, his eyes shut tight in pain, an arrow sticking out of his shoulder.

Chapter 19

Our savages also killed several of them, and took ten or twelve prisoners. The remainder escaped with the wounded. Fifteen or sixteen were wounded on our side with arrow-shots...

—Voyages of Samuel de Champlain

I kneel at Brave One's side and rest my hand on his other shoulder.

"Silent One." He opens his eyes. They are bleary and distant like a sky full of clouds. "Had you spoken, I am guessing you would have told me to stay back." His mouth turns up in the smallest smile, but it quickly turns to another grimace of pain.

I take a knife from my leather pouch – the sharpest I have, with the blade of steel from the Frenchmen's last trading visit—and cut the shaft of the arrow close to his shoulder. The arrow cannot come out now. The bleeding would be too quick, too dangerous. It will have to be secured until we return to our village.

I pull a length of deer sinew from my pouch and use my knife to rip a piece of deerskin from my clothing. With great care, I wrap the skin around my brother's wound and tie it in place with the sinew. I grab what is left of the shaft of the arrow to see if it moves. Brave One winces and closes his eyes, but it is mostly still. He will be able to return with us and be healed back in the village.

I hear the others returning before I see them emerge from the woods.

Champlain leads the pack with his arquebus held high in the air. Etienne and Nicolas scuttle along behind him the way the dogs follow our chiefs in the village.

The air crackles with war cries and whoops and jeers as our warriors lead a dozen Iroquois prisoners back into the clearing.

I watch them, herded like wild beasts.

They are different from us, to be sure. They are Iroquois. Our enemy. They may be the same men who killed Singing Bear and paraded his scalp through their village.

And yet I recognize their eyes. They are full of the same sharp fear I saw in Brave One's eyes not long ago, the same fear I felt prickling my own eyes today.

Brave One groans as I pull him to stand and help him to the edge of the water. He stumbles into our canoe and sinks down into it, grimacing. His face is pale, the war paint washed off with sweat and tears. His chest and stomach are streaked with red. He has lost much blood.

"Not a single man lost!" Champlain declares as he climbs back into his canoe. I do not correct him, but I know it is soon to make that promise.

I have tended to our men after raids before. Battle wounds can steal a man's spirit long after the last arrow has flown.

Chapter 20

After going some eight leagues, towards evening they took one of the prisoners, to whom they made a harangue, enumerating the cruelties which he and his men had already practiced towards them without any mercy, and that, in like manner, he ought to make up his mind to receive as much. They commanded him to sing, if he had courage, which he did; but it was a very sad song.

—Voyages of Samuel de Champlain

Our canoes sit lower in the water as we set out for home.

There is the added weight of our prisoners, bound and loaded into our boats. There is also the corn and meal stolen from the Iroquois village and the armor our men picked up. Our enemies dropped it as they fled in order to run faster.

Brave One rides with Etienne and me. Steps Too Soon accompanies us as well, since his canoe is full of Iroquois captives now. He has said nothing about Brave One's injury—nothing about letting him rush forward on his own. Steps Too Soon paddles with swift, strong strokes and catches up to another boat in which one of the enemy prisoners is held.

"Do you see my friend?" Steps Too Soon asks the Iroquois man, flinging his arm toward Brave One in the front of the canoe. Steps Too Soon spits onto the man in the other boat. "You will be paid back for his wound and for the wrongs you have done to my people. Sing now," he commands.

The Iroquois man's hands and ankles are tied with deer sinew, but he sits up straight. He stares for a long time. Then a low tone grows in his throat, and his mouth opens in song. It is a rhythmic chant, a low voice that mixes with the lapping of the waves, so soft that sometimes it cannot be heard at all.

But he sings.

He stares straight ahead, and he sings. His voice is low, like one I remember from so long ago. He sings to the rhythm of our paddling until Steps Too Soon cuts him off.

"You are brave to sing, to ride along with us without showing your fear. But be prepared for what awaits you. You showed no mercy when Singing Bear was taken from us and killed. We will show you the same before the sun goes down."

The man stops singing. He looks into the eyes of Steps Too Soon but says nothing.

What is there to say?

It is all true. He knows nothing can be said to change the river's course. His fate is as sure as the sunset.

And the sun sinks lower in the sky with every stroke of our paddles.

We have traveled eight leagues, and Champlain motions for us to pull into shore to make camp for the night.

The Iroquois will not follow, he boasts, patting the gun at his side.

We kindle a fire and begin to roast one of the ducks our hunters shot as we paddled back down the lake. The smell makes my mouth water like a dog's. I had not realized how much I'd missed good meat in the days we ate only cold porridge.

When the duck is ready, I tear off a chunk and bring it to Brave One, who rests against an elm.

"You know," he says, biting into the meat with such spirit that the grease runs down his chin, "it was not how I thought."

I hand him a gourd full of water, and he drinks.

"I ran up to the front of the lines with Singing Bear's name on my lips," he says, and he blinks. "But when I pulled back my bowstring, I couldn't let go." He shakes his head. "I wanted revenge in the worst way. I…I miss him so…"

I look away as my eyes water. Brave One does not need to see my tears to know I miss him, too.

"I had aimed perfectly at one of the warriors. An older man. One of the men who has seen many raids. I could tell by his age and the way he carried himself. But I couldn't let the arrow go. He…he reminded me of Singing Bear, and shooting him would have been like shooting…" He sighs. "Do you understand, Brother?"

I do.

But I do not tell him so.

I hand him a wing from the duck, still steaming. He pushes it away with a heavier sigh. "Singing Bear may have been a man who spoke few words. He was a listener; it is true. But he knew when to speak. He knew when someone needed his words. When someone needed a voice to answer his own."

Brave One winces in pain as he pushes himself up against the elm and walks off toward the fire, where the others wait.

But before he leaves, he looks at me once more.

He doesn't turn his head to hide the tears.

Chapter 21

Meanwhile, our men kindled a fire; and, when it was well burning, they each took a brand, and burned this poor creature gradually, so as to make him suffer great torment.

—Voyages of Samuel de Champlain

I wish we were back in the village. I wish I could visit Singing Bear and talk with him about all that has happened.

And I wonder.

Did he see the battle from his place in the spirit world? Was he with us? Was he pleased when the Iroquois war captains fell to Champlain's great gun?

Was he pleased with us?

I whisper my questions to the stars, but they are silent. I know how Brave One feels, pouring out words that never come back.

Finally, I am so hungry I must join the others at the fire.

When I arrive, the copper pot of venison stew hangs on a spit. Its smell drifts out to draw me in.

Etienne sees me coming. "Here," he says, handing me a steaming bowl. "You'll want to step back to eat, I think."

My eyes return to the fire. Some of the men have stuck metal rods deep into the hot coals. They pull them out to check their heat, and when the hot iron glows red, they pull the rods from the fire.

Steps Too Soon holds his in front of him and walks toward one of the Iroquois prisoners, the man he was taunting in the canoe. The man whose quiet song carried our canoes down the lake.

The enemy warrior sits against a rock, his legs bound, his arms tied behind his back. Steps Too Soon reaches forward with the glowing iron rod and presses its tip to the man's bare shoulder.

It sizzles and hisses against his skin. His mouth is drawn tight, but he does not cry out. Steps Too Soon pulls the rod back and extends it toward the man's stomach.

"Wait," says Brave One from his spot next to the fire. As a wounded warrior, he has been given a place of honor at the feast.

Steps Too Soon turns and smiles. "Ah, my brother. You wish to pay this man back for the arrow in your shoulder. Here." He hands the rod to Brave One, who takes it and stares at it the way he stared at the Frenchmen's guns the first time he saw one burst forth with fire and smoke.

"They have lost their leaders and lost their battle," Brave One says quietly. He drops the rod back into the fire and turns away. "I will take no more from them in Singing Bear's name."

Steps Too Soon plunges the rod deeper into the

coals. The firelight flickers in his eyes and makes him look like something that is not quite human. "Your uncle Singing Bear cries for revenge, even tonight." He pulls the rod, brighter still, from the coals. "I can hear him from his place of burial, even now. 'Brave One,' he calls. 'This is the man who must pay for my death. You shall all taste revenge for me tonight!'"

Steps Too Soon opens his mouth and emits something between a whoop and a cackle. He presses the hot iron to the prisoner's chest this time. Bitterness rises in my chest as I cringe and turn away. I do not see, but my ears and nose are assaulted. The same steaming hiss pierces the air. The smell of burned flesh sears into my throat when I inhale.

I join Brave One at the other side of the fire. I do not speak, but I take his hand. We both turn away from the flames, away from the prisoners, as the torture goes on.

I will not turn to look, but still I hear. I imagine the man crying behind me as Singing Bear, and I cannot slow the stream of my tears.

Finally, it grows quiet and I turn back to the fire. My eyes rest on the Iroquois warrior for only a second, but it is long enough to see how he has suffered.

He is splayed on the ground, naked and torn.

Bleeding.

Broken.

And yet he lives. I look back and see his chest rise with a breath.

And then he begins to sing.

It is a low, slow chant. Sad and soft.

And yet he sings.

Steps Too Soon turns back to the prisoner with another rod heated in the fire, but Champlain rises and steps in front of him. He beckons Etienne to his side to translate.

"He says this man has suffered enough," Etienne tells Steps Too Soon, keeping his eyes on the glowing iron rod still clutched in his hands.

"You, too, are merciless to your enemies." Steps Too Soon glares at Etienne. "Why should you tell us how to treat ours?"

"We are fierce warriors, yes," Etienne says, "but we do not torture our enemies like this. We kill them at once." Champlain spoke quickly in Etienne's ear. "He says this man is going to die anyway. Let us kill him with a musket shot that he should suffer no more."

Our warriors murmur to one another. Steps Too Soon steps forward and stretches the hot iron rod toward the prisoner's eye.

Etienne looks at Champlain, who throws up his hands and storms off into the shadows.

The Iroquois man has not moved. And still, he sings.

Steps Too Soon inches the rod closer to his eye.

Still, he sings.

And through his voice, I find my own.

"Stop."

I take a step forward, to catch up to the word that flew from my mouth.

"Stop."

It is just one word. But it seems to have stopped

time. The men stare as if I were a stranger.

"It is enough," I say. My voice is deeper, lower than it was when they last heard me speak.

I say it again. "Stop. Let him shoot the prisoner. Let us show mercy. There has been enough pain today."

I stand and hold out my hand toward Steps Too Soon. He looks at the rod in his hand but does not give it to me.

"I...I had a dream before we met our enemies," I tell them. Every man has turned from the fire to look at me. "In my dream, I was Chaousarou, and there were two Iroquois warriors flying above me. I caught one and devoured him, but the other escaped."

The men watching turn and peer off into the dark woods. They are forever anxious about surprise attacks after a raid.

"I have spoken to Singing Bear at his burial place many times, and I believe he is leading us to a place where we will no longer raid our enemies season after season. To a place where we might live in peace with them."

The men around the fire burst into discussion. Most snort and laugh.

"Ridiculous words from a boy who has no voice. He should have remained silent!" shouts Steps Too Soon, the loudest of them all. He holds the iron rod, still poised near the prisoner's eye.

But our war captain, Wise Elk, steps up beside me. The men grow quiet and wait for him to speak.

A damp log in the fire hisses and pops, and sparks fly up to the sky. I watch until they fade to nothing. And then my eyes settle back on Wise Elk.

"We have not heard the voice of Silent One for many moons." He looks out over the fire, the prisoners, the faces of his own warriors, and me. I look down at the dirt, but he reaches out with rough fingers on my chin and tips my face up toward the men.

"This was a boy who had dreams. Singing Bear told us it was so and promised us a visionary and a healer when he came of age. For reasons we cannot understand, he has not spoken since Singing Bear died. Until tonight."

Wise Elk holds out his hand and stares down at Steps Too Soon. Steps Too Soon hands over the iron rod, and his shoulders fall.

"Tonight," Wise Elk continues, "the boy we called Silent One returns to us as a man. He returns to us with a new voice. And we must listen."

Champlain has come back to the edge of the clearing. Etienne is not there to whisper translations to him, but Wise Elk motions him over to the fire and nods.

The prisoner is still alive. He sings in raspier, quieter breaths.

Wise Elk nods again.

Champlain fires a single musket shot, and he is gone.

Chapter 22

After this execution, we set out on our return with the rest of the prisoners, who kept singing as they went along, with no better hopes for the future than he had had who was so wretchedly treated.

—Voyages of Samuel de Champlain

"He was an Iroquois," Steps Too Soon spits the words into the waves as he paddles. "An Iroquois deserves no mercy."

I do not speak. There is no need. It is done.

We paddle toward home. Brave One is too weak to help. His wound was not deep, but it grows angry and hot and red. He will need medicine soon.

Steps Too Soon pulls his paddle back too far and jars Brave One with his elbow. He winces.

Steps Too Soon does not notice. His eyes fall not on Brave One but on me. "He was probably the very savage who killed Singing Bear. He did not deserve to die so quickly."

"He did not die quickly." I say the words quietly, but my eyes shout. I have had enough.

I pull my paddle more insistently through the current,

trying to push away the dark waters, push away the scenes from the fire. I wish this day were through. Perhaps tomorrow, when Brave One is able to paddle again, Steps Too Soon will move to another canoe.

"He showed bravery, yes," Steps Too Soon says, glaring at me. "You should not have interfered. It is our way. It has always been our way."

"It is not my way."

"And what is your way, Silent One? To sit quietly with our enemy? To steep leaves in water to make him a healing brew? Would you turn away from the man who killed your uncle? Would you not seek revenge in his name? What is your way?"

The wind comes from nowhere and ripples the surface of the lake. My chest still burns with anger at the men who took Singing Bear from me. What do I wish for them? I do not know. I pull harder on my paddle, fighting the waves, saying nothing.

Singing Bear always said it is a foolish man who speaks to a question when he does not know the answer.

By the time the sun sinks toward the earth, we have reached the falls of the Iroquois once again. Here, our Algonquin and Ochateguin warriors leave us. They take with them half of the prisoners, still singing in the ropes that bind them. The warriors carry gifts from the Frenchmen, too—copper kettles, glass beads that glimmer in the sun, and promises that shine.

"He says we shall be pleased to assist you in your future battles against the enemy. We shall continue to be friends and to help one another in this land." Etienne speaks to the departing Algonquin chief. Champlain talks quietly into his ear. "He says together, we are much stronger, and we will be powerful."

The Algonquin chief takes a step back to look at Champlain. His eyes drink in the Frenchman, from the tip of his metal helmet to the heels of his black boots. He nods, but his eyes narrow.

Finally, he turns and leads his men off into the afternoon sun.

Chapter 23

I returned with the Montagnais… When we arrived at the mouth of the river Iroquois, some of the savages dreamed that their enemies were pursuing them. This dream led them to move their camp forthwith, although the night was very inclement on account of the wind and rain; and they went and passed the remainder of the night, from fear of their enemies, amid high reeds on Lake St. Peter.

—Voyages of Samuel de Champlain

We should not have allowed the prisoners to be tortured.

Our hearts were not pure.

I spoke.

But I did not speak soon enough.

Bad spirits follow us.

Brave One grows sicker. He can no longer stand on his own, and red lines of poison streak out from where the arrow pierced his shoulder. Together, Steps Too Soon and I carry him from the canoe and set him under an elm to rest while we make camp.

"I am going to find dogbane," I tell Steps Too Soon, and he nods. Somehow, the fight has drained from his spirit like blood from an open wound. All the men, in fact, seem different today. They step with less confidence now that the fury of battle has settled. They speak in quieter voices as if the cedars, or someone behind the cedars, may be listening.

I walk through the forest until I come to an open creek bed and recognize the white-green flowers of dogbane. They bloom in a patch as long and wide as a canoe, and some of the stalks are taller than I am.

I pluck leaves from the plant, taking care to leave enough that it will still live along the banks and offer help to us on another day.

"The earth will give us what we need," Singing Bear told me as we collected roots one day, "if we remember to give thanks for its gifts." He knelt down to dig the roots of a plant whose yellow bellflowers dripped from its dark green leaves in bunches. It grew at the foot of a giant white pine.

If I close my eyes, I can still smell its pungent needles and feel its cool shadow, even here, where the sun beats down and there is no great pine to offer shade.

I finish gathering the dogbane leaves and tuck them into my pouch. I say a prayer of thanks to the plant and carry the leaves back to the clearing where Brave One now sleeps.

I squat next to him and rest the back of my hand on his forehead. It is as warm as rocks that have been in the sun all day, but he does not sweat.

I hold a gourd to his lips and lift his head. I do not know if he wakes, but he takes a drink. His eyes do not open.

I turn him gently, slowly, so I can see the wound on his shoulder. It oozes yellow fluid, the color of the sky before a storm.

His eyes flutter open.

"Silent One," he whispers through cracking lips.

"I am here."

It is all he needs to know. He drifts back to dreams, and I take the dogbane leaves from my pouch. I use a mortar and pestle to mash them into a sticky green paste, and this I dab onto Brave One's wound.

His mouth twists into a grimace, but he does not cry out.

By the time I finish, it grows dark, and my stomach tells me I must eat.

I stand and turn so quickly I bounce off the big, sturdy chest of Wise Elk. I land hard on my bottom in the dirt, and he reaches down with a big hand to pull me up.

"You know much about healing." He nods down at Brave One, who sleeps quietly again, his chest rising and falling steadily with his breath.

"You know that Singing Bear was teaching me," I tell him. "But he did not have time to finish."

"But you know much."

"I know…some, yes."

"You shall come with me to the fire," he says. "The men have been unsettled all afternoon, like animals in the forest who know hunters are near. They cannot rest but fret and look behind them. There is one who says he has had a dream."

I follow Wise Elk back to the fire, where our warriors

buzz all at once. The loudest of all is Steps Too Soon.

"And in my dream, the enemies followed," he says. He makes a grand, sweeping gesture with his arm and almost knocks another man from the log where he sits. "They came for us, up the lake, past the falls, to a place where the pine trees tower tall over the water."

The men fall quiet. Their eyes drift up to the canopy of cool pine boughs that block the stars from view.

"They follow, I am sure," Steps Too Soon goes on. "We must go back for them and kill every one, or they will pursue us all the way back to our village and murder our wives and children."

The warriors turn to one another, gathering in small, noisy groups. The troubled conversations rise and fall like the crash of waves in a gusty wind. I pick out bits of what they say.

"It must be done, then."

"They follow. It is sure."

"But our scouts—"

"The boy has had a dream."

"He knows."

"He is a child seeking attention."

"But the dream—"

"We must go back and fight again."

"We must."

There are murmurs of agreement, and the small groups join into larger groups as voices lift into the darkening sky.

Wise Elk stands beside me as I listen, and finally, he speaks.

"Have you had a dream?"

"No."

"Do you believe that Steps Too Soon's dream is real?"

I look back at the fire, where Steps Too Soon stands at the center of the warriors, squawking like geese, waving their arms to emphasize their words.

I can tell, without hearing, they are not words of peace.

And yet, to call into question another man's dream does not show respect.

What should I say? Singing Bear's burial place is still so many leagues away, but I send my thoughts out over the water and wait.

The wind whispers through the pines in a gentle whoosh. It is peaceful. It is good.

And I know what I must do.

"I do not know what Steps Too Soon has seen in his dream. I know only what I see in my own mind's eye when sleep carries me off. And I know that we must not fight again now."

The wind settles, and the pine boughs hang silent, listening.

"But you see how uneasy the men are now." Wise Elk tilts his head toward the fire. No one sits. They stand, shifting their weight, pacing back and forth in the orange-red glow. "They believe they are in danger, and we must take them out of that danger so they may rest. Do you agree?"

"We should take them deeper into the forest, then, where there can be no surprise attack from the Iroquois."

Wise Elk puts a hand on my shoulder. "That will

ease their fear," he says, "and fear, now, is a greater threat to us than our enemy."

We spend the rest of the night near another lake. A lake where no one dreams of Iroquois warriors.

A lake where quieter waves lap the shore and pine needles play songs in the breeze.

A lake where tonight, at least, there is peace.

Chapter 24

Two days after, we arrived at our settlement, where I gave them some bread and peas; also some beads, which they asked me for, in order to ornament the heads of their enemies, for the purpose of merry-making upon their return.

　　　　　　　　　—Voyages of Samuel de Champlain

I have traveled far.

I left the fires of Champlain's settlement a boy without a voice.

I return, a young man whose visions have returned. I believe again that I will be a man of healing. A man who speaks.

We must unload the canoes before we can eat.

"Tell him that we must have beads to decorate the scalps," Steps Too Soon is walking so close behind Etienne he has twice tripped over his boots. Still, he leaves no distance. "We fought well, and we should have glass beads."

Etienne stops quickly, and Steps Too Soon crashes into him, knocking his face against Etienne's burly shoulder. The French boy, too, has grown this summer.

His voice was like mine before, like a chipmunk in the woods. Now, it speaks low and strong.

"What is the reason for this savage pageantry?" Etienne turns to me. His eyes are halfway between a fight and a nap. Steps Too Soon has moved on and pesters another Frenchman who clearly does not understand a word he says. He grows more and more annoyed and finally swats Steps Too Soon like a black fly.

I turn back to Etienne and consider his question. What was the reason for our rituals of victory? The reason we would soon parade enemy scalps home as gifts for our women? What was the reason?

"Because it has always been so," I tell him. "Because for as long as this has been our land, they have sent men to raid our village, and we have sent men to raid theirs. Because when you are captured by your enemy, you show bravery, even in death. Because when you win a battle, you return to your village with trophies. Perhaps one day, my people will choose another path."

Steps Too Soon hurries by with the head of an Iroquois warrior, dangling by its long black hair. I watch him pass and turn back to Etienne.

"But for now, this is our way."

We spend two days at the Frenchmen's settlement.

When we first returned, I gave Brave One herbs to make him sleep so I could remove the arrowhead from his shoulder. He bled, but I applied a poultice and wrapped his wound so that he did not lose much more blood. He walks on his own now, for the first time in days. The bad spirits have left him. He joins us at the fire and eats.

We gorge ourselves on fresh meat, on the Frenchmen's bread and beans. We gorge ourselves on chants and songs and victory. And finally, we head for our own village. Finally, we are going home.

Chapter 25

The next day, I went with them in their canoes as far as Tadoussac, in order to witness their ceremonies. On approaching the shore, they each took a stick, to the end of which they hung the heads of their enemies, who had been killed, together with some beads, all of them singing.

—Voyages of Samuel de Champlain

When we approach our village, our warriors hang the heads of our enemies on sticks and attach these to our canoes, so our women will see how victorious we were.

The women rush out to meet us. They laugh and splash in the water. Tears of relief stream from their eyes and spill off their cheeks into the river.

My mother splashes through the current until she reaches our canoe.

"My sons!" she sings. "My sons have returned home from the battle, and I give thanks!" She plucks the Iroquois head from the prow of our canoe and hangs it around her neck. It bounces off her chest as she runs back to shore. She chases Quiet Rain, who not only walks on steady feet but runs now, giggling along the beach. My mother scoops her up and joins the other women to prepare the fire and the feast.

All night long, there is drumming and dancing.

Tonight, I do not have to be coaxed from the side of the fire. I move into the center of the circle, my feet stepping in rhythm with the drums, in rhythm with the hearts of my people. I am home.

Wise Elk steps to the center of the circle, but he does not dance. He raises his hand, and the drums fall silent. The women settle to sit on their heels, and the men step back to the shadows to listen as he gives thanks for our victory.

"Tonight," he says, firelight flickering in his black eyes, "we celebrate a great victory over our enemy. Tonight, we celebrate our return home with all of our warriors, and we give thanks to the spirits that none were lost in this raid."

I step closer to Brave One. His shoulder heals well.

"Tonight, we celebrate the return from battle of warriors who proved their bravery for the first time. Brave One…"

I nudge him forward with my knee. Wise Elk puts a hand on Brave One's good shoulder.

"Brave One stepped forward to fight our enemy. He suffered an arrow wound but has gained a great knowledge. Sometimes, in order to fight bravely, one must step up from the group to lead. Brave One has once again earned the name he was given as a boy."

Brave One steps back, his face flushed.

"Tonight, we celebrate our friends from across the

great waters." Wise Elk holds out a hand to Champlain, who has joined the fire and understands that he, too, should step forward. "We are thankful for your guns that spit fire and show our power to our enemies. We are thankful for your help in battle." He pauses, looks Champlain up and down, and says finally, "We are thankful for your friendship."

Champlain stands looking around until Etienne whispers to him loudly across the crackling flames. Finally, he steps back.

"And tonight," Wise Elk says, "we celebrate the return of one who has been gone from us many moons."

He turns to me, and I step forward.

"He left our village a boy named Silent One. For many moons, he carried great pain in his heart. His spirit was sick and could not speak. But Silent One found his place among us on this journey—his place among warriors and among men.

"Silent One stepped forward to heal his brother's wounds. By this, we were not surprised, for even in his silence, he has been a wise healer, a friend of the medicine plants. On this journey, though, he showed that he will also be one who leads us. And a leader must speak." He looks at me and motions me forward.

I take another step, and before my whole village, before the roaring flames and the stars and the spirit world, I speak.

"I have had a vision," I say, my voice clear as calm water. "In my dream, I heard the voice of Singing Bear once more. He sings for a time when we will no longer raid the Iroquois, when we will fight no more but live as brothers and share the land. It is for Singing Bear that I speak. And for the dream we now share."

I step back into the shadow of a cedar and lean against its cool bark, inhaling the sharp evergreen smell. The men and women buzz with whispers, but Wise Elk holds up his hand once more.

"Tonight, we say goodbye to the boy who left our village, the boy named Silent One. And we celebrate his rebirth. We celebrate his new voice with a new name." He steps toward me. "From here on, you shall be known as Quiet Eagle. An eagle, a creature of leadership and bravery. And quiet, because that boy still lives in you. But remember that quiet does not mean silent. A leader can be quiet. But sometimes he must speak. And when a true leader speaks, the people will listen."

Wise Elk steps back into the shadows. Drumbeats rise up out of the earth again, louder and louder, until I feel them shake my heart.

I am almost ready to dance.

But first, I must pay a visit.

I tuck some venison into my pouch and turn from the fire.

My feet keep time with the drumming, the chanting, as I run off through the trees to the place I have run away to so many times before.

Tonight, my footsteps pound a different beat. I run toward a new beginning.

"Uncle," I whisper through the hole in the burial hut. "I am thankful for your voice, for it guided me through

the country of the Iroquois. Even there, I felt your presence, like a hand on my arm, like a star in the sky."

The breeze gathers into a real wind, and the trees sway in the clearing. I pull my fur closer around me. The air on our journey was thick and wet and warm, but tonight, it feels like the leaves will change color any day.

"I am thankful for your gift of healing," I whisper, "for it saved Brave One from bad spirits that made him burn and cry out. I am thankful for the voice you returned to me when I was so far from home."

I pull the dried venison from my pouch and push little pieces through the opening.

The wind blows harder. Leaves rustle over my head. They whisper songs of hope. Songs of a lasting peace.

They speak to me, but I cannot make out their words. Only their message.

A leader cannot be silent.

The message of Wise Elk and Singing Bear. The message I will carry to my people.

One day, a leader will speak for peace. And the people will listen.

I push the last of the venison through the hole and start back to the fire. Drumbeats and chants rise over the treetops and carry me along.

It is time to dance.

Author's Note

While this story is based on the actual voyage of Samuel de Champlain in 1609, Silent One is a fictional character. There were, in fact, Native American guides with Champlain when he made his famous journey, but their names, ages, and other personal information were not recorded. Some of those guides, like Silent One, were members of the Innu tribe, which the French called Montagnais.

In fact, the only written record of this voyage comes from Champlain himself, and historians recognize that even the most detailed recorders tend to portray historical events with their own biases. Silent One's story is a work of fiction. It is my own representation of what an Innu boy traveling with Champlain might have thought of the events recorded in Champlain's journal and what he might have thought of Champlain himself.

I have tried to be as accurate as possible in portraying the culture and lifestyle of Silent One and his people, but again, written records of the Native culture of this time period are scarce. Of course, Silent One would not have spoken English, but this is the language in which you're reading his story. In the interest of understanding for modern readers, I have used some English words and concepts that do not translate into the Innu language. Some of these are fascinating. The Innu, for example, had no general word for tree—only words for specific species like elm, cedar, oak, etc. The Innu words I've used in this story come from a Innu language website that you can visit to learn more about the language (http://www.innu-aimun.ca).

The characters of Etienne and Nicolas are based on two real young men who were part of Champlain's party—Etienne Brule and Nicolas Marsolet. Both served as translators in New France, and both survived the brutal winter of 1609, though there is no evidence they were actually with Champlain on his voyage south, as they are in this story. Nicolas, in fact, spent most of his time at the original Innu village in Tadoussac. The real Etienne Brule was a notorious rebel and did eventually leave the Frenchmen to join the Hurons.

After the battle, Champlain and most of his men traveled back to France. The Indians sent them home with many beaver pelts, an Iroquois scalp, and a head of the great fish, Chaousarou.

But the story does not end there. Champlain returned to the New World, along with more French men and women. It is true that in fighting the Iroquois that summer of 1609, Champlain gained the friendship of the Innu, Huron, and Algonquin. But he also made enemies. The Iroquois aligned themselves with the British in the

Hudson Valley, and together, they eventually drove the French from the region in what we now call the French & Indian Wars. Battles over Lake Champlain and the land surrounding it continued through the American Revolution and the War of 1812.

Though the Algonquin and Innu initially profited from their friendship with the French, the benefit was not a lasting one. As the wars over land raged and more European settlers came to the New World, the Algonquins and Innu were forced further and further from their traditional hunting ground. Finally, like so many other tribes of North America, they lost virtually all of the land they had called home for generations.

Voices like Silent One's have been silenced in many times and places, but they echo through history as a reminder that we can all speak for peace.

There can never be peace between nations until there is first known that true peace which is within the souls of men.

–Black Elk, a holy man of the Oglala Lakota, 1932

About the Author

Kate Messner is a writer and middle school English teacher living on Lake Champlain with her husband and kids. Her first book, *Spitfire*, won the 2007 Adirondack Literary Award for Children's Literature.

Visit Kate at her website:
www.katemessner.com

References

If you would like to explore the history behind *Champlain and the Silent One*, there are many outstanding books, websites, and museums where you can learn more. Here are some that you might enjoy:

Livesey, Robert and A.G. Smith. *The Fur Traders (Discovering Canada)*. Allston, MA: Fitzhenry & Whiteside, 1989.

Livesey, Robert and A.G. Smith. *New France (Discovering Canada)*. Allston, MA: Fitzhenry & Whiteside, 1990.

Morganelli, Adrianna. *Samuel de Champlain: From New France to Cape Cod*. New York: Crabtree Children's Books, 2005.

Lake Champlain Maritime Museum
http://www.lcmm.org

References

Canadian Museum of Civilization
   http://www.civilization.ca/visit/indexe.aspx

National Museum of the American Indian
   http://www.nmai.si.edu

For Further Reading

The following sources were invaluable in my research for *Champlain and the Silent One*.

Bellico, Russell. *Chronicles of Lake Champlain: Journeys in War and Peace*. Fleischmanns, NY: Purple Mountain Press, 1999.

Champlain, Samuel de, Charles P. Otis, and Edmund F. Slafter. *Voyages of Samuel de Champlain* (English translation). Boston: The Prince Society, 1878-1882.

Cronon, William. *Changes in the Land: Indians, Colonists, and the Ecology of New England*. New York: Hill and Wang, 1983.

Eccles, W.J. *The French in North America: 1500-1783*. Marham, Ontario: Fitzhenry & Whiteside, 1998.

Leacock, Eleanor. *The Montagnais Hunting Territory and the Fur Trade*. Menasha, WI. American Anthropological Association, 1954.

Mann, Charles C. *1491: New Revelations of the Americas Before Columbus*. New York: Alfred A. Knopf, 2005.

Moogk, Peter N. *La Nouvelle France: The Making of French Canada—A Cultural History*. East Lansing, MI: Michigan State University Press, 2000.

Parkman, Francis. *France and England in North America, Vol. 1*. New York: Library of America, 1983.

Pritchard, Evan T. *No Word for Time: The Way of the Algonquin People*. San Francisco: Council Oak Books, 2001.

Richter, Daniel K. *Facing East from Indian Country: A Native History of Early America*. Cambridge, MA: Harvard University Press, 2001.

Sagard, Father Gabriel. *The Long Journey to the Country of the Hurons*. Edited by George M Wrong. Toronto: The Champlain Society, 1939.

Trigger, Bruce R. *The Children of Aataentsic I: A History of the Huron People to 1660*. Montreal: McGill-Queens University Press, 1976.